DEVIOUS SECRET

BRENTSON UNIVERSITY
BOOK 2

BRI BLACKWOOD

BRETAGEY PRESS

NOTE FROM THE AUTHOR

Hello!

Thank you for taking the time to read this book. Devious Secret is a dark college billionaire enemies-to-lovers romance. It is not recommended for minors and contains situations that are dubious and could be triggering. The book also includes graphic violence, kidnapping, vomiting, and brief mentions of a mental disorder which might also be triggering. It isn't a standalone and the book ends in a cliffhanger. The next book in the series is Devious Heir.

BLURB

I should have stayed gone...
But I was lured back by the promise of getting closure.
Now I'm being held captive by my ex,
Who has no intention of letting me go.
He believes he knows everything about me.
But what he doesn't know is
That I have a secret.
And I intend to take it to the grave.

PLAYLIST

Prisoner — Miley Cyrus, Dua Lipa

Colors — Halsey

Boys Will Be Boys — Dua Lipa

Cry About It Later — Katy Perry

I'm Ready — Sam Smith, Demi Lovato

Sour Candy — Lady Gaga, BLACKPINK

Happiness — Little Mix

What I've Done — Linkin Park

Guess I'm a Liar — Sofia Carson

Secret (Pretty Little Liars Theme) — Denmark +Winter

The playlist can be found on Spotify.

1

NASH

The thrill of a kill was something I would never get over. It created this feeling that I could barely describe. It caused the blood pumping through my veins to feel as if it were on fire. I was still riding the high from killing Paul because he stalked Raven and would be for a while yet.

There was something else though. Something other than the intoxicating feeling of taking someone's life was there, even though it was someone who deserved it. It took me a second to narrow it down, but when I finally did, I knew it was rage. Rage that I'd suppressed from when I found out that Raven had left Brentson. Rage that grew stronger, darker, after the explanation for that departure that I received from my father.

Raven denied what my father said was true just before she tried to escape, but I didn't believe her. Now, while my relationship with my father wasn't all sunshine and roses, mostly because of his selfishness, I don't think he would ever try to intentionally hurt me. I could not say the same thing about Raven. If she had no issue with leaving town without saying a word to the person she supposedly loved, then why should I believe her now? Plus, his explanation for what happened would be an excellent reason to leave Brentson. I would be ashamed if I'd done the same thing.

I didn't bother to ask my father for details of the encounter because it wasn't something that I wanted to live through. Even now, the mental image that I'd formed was enough to piss me off all over again. Knowing that she betrayed my trust and our relationship and then skipped town hurt like hell every day. It had been like a punch to the gut that I still wasn't completely over.

Attempting to sleep with one of the most important political figures in this town, a man who also happened to be your boyfriend's father, was a special kind of low. Scratch that. It was a special kind of fucked up, which is why her disappearance made sense.

Thinking about what occurred right after my high school graduation forced me to relive how distraught I'd been. My father's version of events added gasoline to the fire that had become my rage. To make matters worse, while I was angry at her and the situation she had caused, I still cared about her. And that just pissed me off even more.

At first, I'd been in denial about everything. There was no way my Raven could have done what she'd been accused of doing. I wanted to call the police because I was worried about Raven's well-being. I remembered wondering every morning if today would be the day she would reach out and, at the very least, tell me that she was all right. But that day never came.

Over the years, I fought through thoughts that she'd somehow gotten hurt or died whenever they filtered into my consciousness. On several occasions, I'd asked Izzy if she'd heard from Raven, but she'd always denied knowing anything. I had to respect her loyalty, even though it had caused me a world of pain.

I clenched the steering wheel in my hands as I navigated us away from Brentson while I tried to remove the negative thoughts from my mind. Instead, I decided to think about the path that was ahead of me. I knew we wouldn't be returning for a few days. Plans needed to be made quickly. There was a lot to do in such a short amount of time.

Most importantly, we were driving away from our past and our present, and toward a future that was unknown. And in order for this to happen, I'd kidnapped her. That might not have been the best way forward, but it was necessary. Okay, even I had to admit that was also pretty fucked up.

I removed one hand from the steering wheel to brush it back through my hair. After the events that occurred tonight, driving would be therapeutic for me. This ride would give me the opportunity to calm down in peace. In a messed-up way, it was actually for the best that Raven was knocked out because the energy that coursed through me right now couldn't be controlled. I couldn't deal with her like this. I wouldn't be able to control my reactions to her.

Weirdly enough, out of all the things that happened this evening, the most eerie one for me was driving down this road with Raven in the car, fleeing the scene of the destruction that we caused. It made me feel as if I'd slipped into the position she'd taken when she left town over two years ago.

Shaking those memories and thoughts from my head, I

tried to focus on everything that went wrong today. I'd certainly had no plans to murder a man when the day began. None of this was what I thought would happen, but the saying about how screwed up the best-laid plans could become would definitely apply here. Things really didn't go wrong, though, but I did have to pivot in order to get what I wanted.

What I wanted was to get revenge. What I got was blood on my hands and an ex that I'd had no choice but to kidnap. But if I hadn't arrived at Raven's place when I did, the chances of her being in the back of that fucker's SUV were high. I'd fought him off and made sure he hadn't succeeded, and in the back of my mind, I knew I wasn't remotely innocent. And I would do it all again without shame.

There were things that you needed to do in order to become a member of the Chevaliers. Things I wouldn't admit to anyone I deemed unworthy of knowing. But I'd done them because that was what was required of me. It was what I needed to do to get to where I wanted to go and that now put me on track to being one of the last people standing for the chairmanship of one of the most coveted branches of this organization in the world.

I looked at Raven, slouched over with her head leaning against the window. She looked so peaceful in her sleep, and there was a small part of me that enjoyed watching her like this as it brought back memories of when she would fall asleep while we were watching TV at her mother's place.

However, this was just the calm before the storm. I knew that once she woke up and remembered what I'd done, all hell would be unleashed. I would have to deal with her wrath and, honestly, most of me wanted all of that fire and rage. There was a chance she'd never understand what I'd done, and that was something I was willing to live with.

Kidnapping her was the best option I had to get us both out of this situation safely. Well, I suppose safely was a relative term given the state she was in. Deep down, I knew I should have some remorse for knocking her out, but I didn't. I was known for going above and beyond to achieve my goals and this was no exception. It was also one of the qualities that made me a great Chevalier and worthy of competing for chairmanship.

Thinking of these trials as if they were a competition wasn't right but that's always where my mind landed. I was in this to become chairman, and anything less would be considered a failure. I'd worked hard since I joined the Chevaliers, and I would make sure that it wouldn't be in vain. It might sound cliché, but failure wasn't an option.

I pressed a button and the volume of the classic soft rock station increased. Having some music on in the background would help quiet my brain. It wasn't the type of music I regularly listened to, but I learned within the last couple of years that it had calming effects on me. I needed this to clear my mind so I could properly think about the next steps.

What had been easy for me to decide was that we needed to get out of town. I was driving us farther north to a small cabin that Bianca and I inherited from our grandfather when he passed away. I tended to use the cabin more than she did, and it was secluded enough that, unless you were actively looking for the property, the likelihood of anyone coming across it was low.

It would be the perfect place to keep Raven. With that covered, I could figure out what to do next.

My parents owned the adjacent piece of property and there was a huge, luxurious cabin that we had the option to use. My grandfather had intended for the larger cabin to be used for the family gatherings that my grandmother always loved to have. She very much believed in keeping the family close-knit and connected with one another, so my grandfather's idea had been perfect. However, she passed away before she could see the cabin completed. Now, the main cabin had a full-time staff in case my parents or other extended family were hosting visitors there, or if anyone wanted to get away for a couple of days, but it was rarely used.

The smaller cabin was built by my grandfather once my grandmother died because it helped with his grief. While there was the option for us to stay at the larger cabin on the property because I believed it was currently vacant, I thought it best to choose the one I owned. There was nowhere that Raven could run, and over the time that we'd spend here, we'd be forced to deal with the issues we had with one another.

As soon as we reached the cabin, there would be a number of phone calls that I needed to make. Each one would play an intricate role in keeping what I was doing a secret. If, in the end, all of this meant I would finally get the answers I was looking for and keep Raven safe, then it was well worth it.

The soft rock music and the low murmur from my GPS every so often guided me down the dark roads until I saw the lights of the Henson family cabin welcoming me. It would have been easier for me to make a pitstop at the main lodge to check off the first task on my list, but I decided to keep driving. I didn't want to risk stopping and Raven waking up alone in an empty car and doing who knows what.

A couple of turns down a less-paved road led me to my grandfather's cabin. The well-kept home was nowhere near the showstopper that the family cabin was, but it was nice and cozy. It was a perfect fit for a man who needed a place to retreat to where the chances of him getting bothered were slim.

I brought the car to a stop and threw it into park. I looked over at Raven to see if my stopping the car had roused her, but she didn't move. It took no time for me to step out of the car, walk up the front porch stairs, and open the front door of the cabin. I quickly turned on the lights and double checked that there was nothing obstructing me from getting into the bedroom before walking back outside. When I reached the passenger side door, I took a deep breath and hoped she wouldn't wake up while I was trying to bring her into the house. If she did, I knew it would lead to a fight I didn't want to have right now, especially not out here. I opened the door and made quick work of undoing her seatbelt and pulled her toward me so I could carry her inside.

Having her in my arms in any way possible seemed to be what I constantly strived for nowadays.

The trip from my car to the bedroom lasted less than a few minutes, but every second that ticked by, I wondered if this would be the moment Raven woke up. I laid her down on the bed and cursed to myself when I realized I hadn't turned down the bed before I put her on it. There was no way in hell

I was going to risk waking her up in order to put the bed's covers over her body.

I stood up and looked around the room. It took me a second to spot the blanket folded up on one of the armchairs in the room. I walked over to the chair, grabbed the blanket, and turned around to drape it over Raven's body. That would have to do for right now.

I took a step back to see if she was going to stir after I'd laid the blanket on her. When she didn't, I walked away from her and closed the bedroom door in an attempt to not wake her while I did other things.

The first place I stopped was the kitchen. I looked through the refrigerator, small pantry, and cabinets and found that while there were some unexpired nonperishables —there wasn't much else. We would need a lot more food than this.

I pulled my phone out of my pocket as I strolled into the living room. I ended up stopping at my grandfather's wooden desk. It was much smaller than the one he'd put in the main cabin, but efficient enough for what I wanted to use it for. I glanced at some of the books he'd left there that gave a window into the things he liked. A couple of thrillers, crossword puzzle books, and a book on the Chevaliers. I picked up the Chevalier book and flipped through it. We knew that this wasn't the only book on the Chevaliers that my grandfather owned, but it was the only one that we could currently find. Normally, this kind of book wouldn't appeal to me, but maybe I should take the opportunity to read through it while I was here.

I couldn't help but think of how much my grandfather enjoyed being out here, and it gave him the seclusion he craved at times. Now it would do the same for Raven and me for the time being.

I ran a hand across the wooden surface as I searched my phone's contacts for the first person I needed to call.

It was time to get to work.

2

RAVEN

I could feel myself starting to wake up, but I wished I wouldn't. Waking up was too painful. The throbbing in my head felt as if someone was playing the drums nonstop, but that wasn't the only thing that felt strange and hurt. No matter how many times I swallowed, the metallic taste in my mouth refused to go away. I was way too tired and the desire to stay asleep was there, but something was forcing me awake.

Mama?

No, that wasn't right. Mama died years ago. What the hell was wrong with me?

I was, without a doubt, disoriented. There was no question about it because I couldn't remember the last time that I'd forgotten that my mother was no longer alive. There had been a few moments after she died where I'd woken up thinking that it was all a nightmare, but my reality had been worse. Tears formed behind my closed eyelids. Thinking about my mother's death always led to them.

I felt as if I'd been body slammed at some point and then

proceeded to get hit by a two by four upside the head repeatedly. If I was being honest, I wasn't sure how accurate my assumption was. I tried to move my head to the side and swallowed hard. The pain almost took my breath away. Instead of trying to move my head again, I tried to move my hand. It was a struggle to move it also, and when I did, a dull ache shot through my arm. I winced, but the ache subsided as quickly as it started. *Had I laid on my hand wrong or had something more dire happened?*

When I tried to move my hand a second time, it wasn't painful, which was encouraging. Now that I could move my hand around more freely, I felt around and came into contact with something that felt like a blanket.

That normally wouldn't be an issue for me except I knew that neither of the two blankets I owned felt like this. I moved my hand and clenched the sheets. They felt thicker than the ones I had on my bed.

The need to find out what the hell was going on won me over. I started to panic, and I was willing to risk more pain to get the answers I desired. Although it was easier said than done, I slowly opened my eyes. Tears slowly drifted down my cheeks and I did nothing to stop them.

The first thing that hit me was the sun shining in through the window closest to me. How was it daylight already when the last thing I remembered was it being nighttime? How long had I been asleep?

What time was it?

My eyes studied the room I was in. Although I'd already thought that something was wrong based on how the bedding felt, confirming it sent a shock through my already fragile system. I recognized nothing about the room. The art on the walls, the heavily wooden aesthetic—that seemed to be a design feature throughout the room—was all new to me.

None of this makes sense. Where the hell am I?

I slowly turned my head to the left and to the right, taking in what I could as I tried to find anything that looked familiar. I didn't see anything that I recognized. The only thing I was able to figure out was that I was in a bedroom, laying on a bed. The room itself didn't include much else outside of a fireplace and two dark red chairs on the opposite side of it.

I moved my limbs again and was relieved to discover that I wasn't tied down. Panic again surged through me as I realized I had no recollection of how I got into this room. The only option that was left was I had to have been brought here by someone, but who?

I tried to sit up and collect myself, but nausea took over. When I tried to take deep breaths to calm it down, it only grew worse.

I closed my eyes, convinced that I'd seen enough for the time being. It wasn't like it was helping anyway. After a few seconds and several more deep breaths, I slowly turned my head and saw what looked to be a bathroom sink and mirror. It was through a doorway diagonally across from where I was laying. I slowly laid back down and closed my eyes, hoping to get some strength to make a run for it, because now I knew, without a doubt, I was going to throw up.

Although I had been able to calm my queasy stomach somewhat, the urge to vomit was still too strong. I knew this was my chance to make it to the next room. Trying to figure out where I was would have to wait, because the only thing on my mind was getting into the bathroom as fast as possible. I took another deep breath and threw the blanket off of my body. I eased into a sitting position, moving my legs so that my feet could touch the floor. I stood up and that set off a chain of events. My nausea rose with a vengeance and hit me, much like the throbbing in my head. I had no choice but to run across to the doorway and hope that I was right in my guess about it being a bathroom.

My hand flew over my mouth as I power walked the distance to the doorway. Thankfully, I found a light to illuminate the room before it started spinning. While I felt like hell, relief flowed through me at being right and finding the bathroom. It only lasted a second, though, because now I was kneeling over the toilet and throwing up my stomach's contents.

I found myself saying repeatedly in my mind that I wished this was over. It had become my mantra, one that I hoped would come true sooner rather than later. My hand moved to tuck my hair behind my ears in an attempt to avoid making a bigger mess that I would eventually have to clean up. The violent motions my body was going through made me feel absolutely miserable. It felt like I was hacking up every organ in my body.

When my throwing up slowed enough to allow me to finally catch my breath, I was grateful for the reprieve. As I took in big gulps of air, I wasn't surprised to find a tear falling down my face, and I knew there would be more to come. Within seconds, there was no stopping the tears from streaming down my face.

Here I was, so damn close to bawling in a bathroom and I had no idea where I was, or who or what else was here. As if I'd spoken my internal thoughts out loud, I saw movement out of the corner of my eye. I was too afraid to move my head to look over to see what it was, in case it would lead to round two of this hell. Instead, I focused on closing my eyes and letting my body do what it needed to do, which, right now, was taking deep breaths. It wasn't until I felt someone lightly grab my hair that I bothered to spare a glance.

Nash.

Miraculously, seeing him didn't cause me to throw up again. I actually hated how good he looked right now, whereas I knew I had to have looked like something out of a horror movie. As I tried to recover and gather my bearings, memories flooded my mind. I remembered watching Nash murder the man who'd tried to kidnap me, escaping Chevalier Manor, and running through the woods. Things became fuzzy after that, but my intuition told me that something wasn't right. I wanted to tell Nash to let go of my hair, however, fighting him would only exert more energy than I had.

All of this was humiliating. Maybe it was my karma that I had to have him witness me throwing up and having him help me, but there was nothing I could do about it now. With a sigh, I lightly pulled on my hair, indicating that I wanted him to let it go. Once he did, I reached up so I could flush the toilet. When that task was done, I shifted my body, so my back was against the wall. I closed my eyes and sat there, focusing on taking deep breaths.

Deep breath in and out.

When I had more confidence that I wasn't going to end up kneeling in front of the toilet again, I opened my eyes and held out my hand. "Can I get a towel?"

Nash said nothing, but to my surprise, he listened to me. He reached over and grabbed a hand towel that had been draped along a rack on the wall. After he handed it to me, he stood up. "I'm going to get you a cool washcloth to place on your head too."

"I don't remember asking for that," I replied.

"Tough shit," he said. "You don't have much of a choice, do you now, Little Bird?"

I didn't respond because I didn't have one. He was right. I was at his mercy right now.

He made no effort to turn around and look at me. The harshness in his reply didn't surprise me. While it did bother me to have to ask for his help, I had no choice, so I tried to not let it get to me.

I watched as he walked over to a small closet in the bathroom and grabbed a washcloth before he turned on the faucet. Once the washcloth was wet, he wrung it out and walked over to me again.

"Take the washcloth, Raven."

My eyes widened when he said my first name. More memories came back to me. I remembered the last time he said my first name was when I was trying to escape from his car. My hand shook slightly as the realization hit and he placed the wet washcloth in my hand.

"You kidnapped me," I said. My voice barely above a whisper.

"I did." He didn't even try to deny it.

"What did you use to knock me out?"

"Chloroform."

"And you just have something like that lying around in your car, ready to use at a moment's notice? I could have died!"

If I had died, it wouldn't have been the only murder he

committed that night. I kept that bit to myself and instead chose to close my eyes again and tried to calm my racing heart. I was getting worked up and that was a sure-fire way for me to end up getting sick again. Nash didn't reply, which was very fitting for him.

There were so many questions I wanted to ask, but I couldn't find the strength to do so. It was as if my body realized that I was exhausted again. I was sure I could fall back asleep, right here, right now. I continued to allow my body to rest against the wall with my eyes closed.

I didn't keep track of how long I'd stayed in that position, but for the time being, it was where I felt most comfortable. Mentally, I made plans to move, but my body told me that it wouldn't be any time soon.

Nash cleared his throat, forcing my eyes to open and drawing my attention back to him. "Come on."

"I'm okay resting right here."

"But for how long? I'll pick you up and take you back to bed."

I debated trying to put up a bigger fight but decided not to. It wouldn't help, and I'd probably start throwing up again. Besides, the pounding in my head wasn't getting any better either. He bent down and picked me up. I tightened my grip on both the washcloth and the towel and threw one arm around his neck in an attempt to better anchor myself to his body as he carried me back into the bedroom.

He laid me down on the bed and placed the compress on my forehead. The cooling sensation felt wonderful on my feverish skin. Normally, I would have profusely thanked the person who'd done this for me but the anger I still had for Nash clouded any reminder about the manners I had.

I watched as he tucked me into bed. It wasn't until he was pulling the covers over me that I realized the bed had been turned down. He must have done it quickly when I was in the bathroom.

Nash walked back into the bathroom and came out with a trash can and sat it on the floor near the bed. He gave me one final look before walking out of the room and closing the door behind him. It took a couple of minutes before I felt confident that he wasn't coming back. I closed my eyes to relax and hopefully fall asleep.

In my mind, none of his actions since I'd woken up canceled out what he'd done. The urge to fight back was still there. If I could have trusted that my body would withstand the exertion, I would have put up a fight and done my best to find a way to break out. It would be foolish to attempt to escape in my current state.

But when I was strong enough?

Nothing was going to stop me from getting out of here and reporting Nash to the police, even if it meant that I had to go down with him.

NASH

"Thank you."

"It was no problem, sir."

As I closed and locked the front door of the cabin, I thought about how this half-assed idea might actually work. At the very least, we would have enough food to sustain us for our stay. I started unpacking the food I'd gotten from the main cabin. It had taken a couple of hours for our staff to put together several meals and snacks so all I needed to do was heat them up. I'd asked them not to mention that I was here in order to give Raven and me some privacy from the people who knew about the small cabin's existence.

Once I'd had all the food put away, I walked back toward the bedroom. I slowly twisted the doorknob, doing my best to softly open the door, in hopes that I wouldn't disturb Raven if she was still sleeping. It turned out that she was.

I couldn't help but to stare at her lying there peacefully. I knew that her getting sick had taken a lot out of her, and I did have some guilt about being the reason for it. But even with all of the shit that happened, I couldn't get over how beautiful she looked.

With that beauty, came a stubbornness like I'd never seen before. It had been easy to tell that it pained her to have to rely on my help when I found her in the bathroom, but she didn't have any other options beside me at the moment. And it was all my fault. Would I have changed the way I'd done things now? Yes, but only if it meant that she wouldn't be suffering.

When I came in to check on her last night, maybe an hour after we'd arrived, she was restless. She would twist and turn in her sleep even though it caused her pain. At least she had some relief now, but I knew it was only temporary. Once she woke up and had to deal with the ramifications of what occurred last night, it would be a completely different story. From her almost being kidnapped by Paul, to seeing me kill the man who had attempted to kidnap her, to me whisking her away to my private little getaway.

The one thing that made me feel better about everything that happened was that she was finally getting the rest she needed. What she had been through was dramatic by itself and it was only made worse because of the other circumstances and questions that we didn't know the answers to. I still couldn't get her denial of my father's explanation for her disappearance out of my mind. For now, my desire to find out why she left and why she returned would have to wait until we moved past this hurdle.

I pushed those thoughts to the side because I had a few other priorities I needed to take care of in the meantime. I made a mental note to myself that I would put the lasagna— one of the dishes that was prepared for us and what used to be one of Raven's favorite foods—in the oven. There was also a soup that I could throw together if Raven wasn't up to eating something as heavy as lasagna. I had the feeling she would make do with the lasagna, even if soup was the better option, because of her love for it. Well, if that was still the case.

If she wasn't awake by the time our meal was done cooking, then I would wake her up so we could eat together. That gave me plenty of time to contact everyone I needed to reach out to. I picked up my phone and called Easton, because he would need time to be able to drive out here.

"Yo," he said when he answered my call.

"Are you busy?"

"Nah. I'm done with my classes for today. Why? What do you need?"

"I need you to stop by my place and then head to Raven's. I'll send you a list of things to grab and drive it over here to me."

I heard some shuffling in the background and it took Easton a moment before he responded.

"Wait, why? Where the hell are you?"

"I'll send you the address and then when you get here, I'll give you further directions."

"I'm going to need more information than that and you know it. What the hell is going on?"

"Look, I won't be on campus for a few days, and I need some things from my apartment because I didn't have time to grab them before I left."

"Why does this sound like a secret ops mission?"

This time, I rolled my eyes. He wasn't right, but I wouldn't say he was wrong either. "Can you do it or not?"

"Yes. Text me the address and what you need, and I'll swing by both of your homes and get it."

"Thanks."

"But I also want to know what is going on."

"Fine. We'll discuss it when you get here."

I hung up and knew that I couldn't give him all of the details about what was going on and bring him into this shit because he wasn't a Chevalier. I had a sneaky suspicion that he wanted to become one, but he'd never said those words to me, so I left it alone. I scrolled through my phone's contact list before I found the number I needed to call.

"Nash."

It was a little jarring hearing Tomas say my name instead of a greeting, but I went along with it.

"I wanted to let you know that I will be off campus for the next few days."

"Does this have anything to do with the killing of the man you left in Chevalier Manor for us to clean up?"

I winced. I had left a mess for them to deal with, but I highly doubted Tomas got his hands messy in the cleanup.

"I apologize for that. I had something I needed to take care of...something I still need to take care of."

I wasn't sure how much he knew about my current situation, and I wasn't sure how much he needed to know.

"It's Raven, isn't it?"

My silence was the only confirmation he needed.

"The only reason why I remotely care about this is because you brought this mess to our home, Nash."

"I did it because it was the only place that I knew where I would be able to handle this situation easily."

"I was easy on you when I saw you that night because I

didn't want to embarrass you in case you do become chairman." He sighed. "If this will lead you to completing the task in your envelope, then so be it."

There was no way that Tomas would have been able to embarrass me because based on the way I felt that night, I would have had no issue taking all of the men in that room on after I killed Paul. I felt that fucking powerful. But I was surprised by his compassion about the chairman trials. "What do you mean by that?"

He paused for a beat and then said, "You're going to miss one of our meetings. And don't forget you still have duties as a Chevalier. This doesn't count the tasks you need to complete in order to be a consideration for chairman."

It was as if I hadn't asked a question and that irritated me, to put it mildly. "You didn't answer my question."

I did my best not to question the Chevalier leadership because it had been an unspoken rule, but I wasn't about to let Tomas get away with this.

"I know I didn't. It's because you aren't ready for the answer yet."

"Wait a damn—"

It took everything within me to calm that reaction. Every expletive I could think of was hanging out on the tip of my tongue, ready to fly free, but I swallowed my pride and held back. There were bigger things at play here and I needed to remember that. I waited for Tomas to respond.

"Trust me on this, even if you don't trust me regarding anything else, Nash. You already know part of the reason why Raven's name was in your envelope. Once you connect the dots, it will become clearer. Now, back to what I was saying about you missing a Chevalier meeting."

"I know. And I promise I will find a way to make it work. I do have one clarifying question though."

Tomas cleared his throat. "Yes?"

"Do any of the events of the last twenty-four hours affect my chances of becoming chairman?" I wanted to know what I was up against. If what I was currently dealing with set me back in any way, I wanted to know so I could better prepare myself for what I needed to do next.

Tomas didn't answer right away. The silence that passed between us seemed like a lifetime. "I'll double check with the others, but as far as it stands with me, you're fine. These are extraordinary circumstances beyond your control. Just make sure you're available for the next round of trials."

"Thank you, Chairman."

My phone buzzed in my hand. I pulled my phone away from my ear and found that it was a call from my father. I pressed ignore and continued to wrap up my conversation with Tomas.

"And one more thing."

"Yes?" I waited for him to say what I assumed would be the last thing he needed to say.

"You asked leadership why Raven's name was inside your envelope."

"Right."

"Out of all the reasons in the world, why would it make sense for Raven's name to be in your envelope? You should think about it that way."

His answer confused me, but I knew that this was the end of the call. "Uh. Thank you."

"Good. I'll see you soon."

"Bye."

Tomas ended the call, and I was left staring at my phone, racking my brain as I tried to process what happened. It had gone better than I had anticipated, but I still got the sneaky suspicion that I wasn't completely in the clear.

Then it hit me like a lightning bolt. What had been made clear was why Raven's name had been written on a piece of paper that had been placed in my envelope. It was because she was my biggest weakness.

4

———

RAVEN

I couldn't help but smile as Nash pulled his car to a stop outside of one of my favorite places on Earth. My excitement refused to be contained. "I didn't know you were bringing us here!"

"That's because it was a surprise," Nash said. "Think of it as a treat after a long week of school."

He wasn't wrong. We were three weeks into the start of our senior year of high school. The amount of work that we'd already been given had been a lot to wrap our brains around, so this was a welcomed surprise. I smiled at him and looked back at the sign outside the car window. I didn't think I would ever forget the design of Smith's Ice Cream Parlor. With its red, fancy lettering on a white background and a graphic of a sundae tied into its logo, it was easily identifiable, and I could feel my body's happiness at what it was about to digest.

I was so grateful that Nash decided to surprise me with ice cream from one of the best dessert places in this region. So many people came from near and far to try Smith's famous ice cream. We *were fortunate to have it in our town, making it easier to visit whenever we wanted.*

"Come on, let's go."

I paused as I watched Nash undo his seatbelt and exit the car. Before he could get to my side, I quickly unstrapped myself and opened my door. When I stepped out to meet him, Nash gave me a playful glare that said he didn't approve of me doing that. He was usually the one that opened my door when I was with him, and he'd always give me shit when I did it myself. He shook his head as the glare left his face and a smile appeared on his lips.

Nash held out his hand for me to grab. With our hands intertwined, we walked into Smith's and ordered our favorite flavor of ice cream. I smiled when Nash handed me a cone of birthday cake ice cream, and he'd chosen cookies and cream for himself.

We picked a small table near a window and spent a couple of seconds enjoying our ice cream before I spoke.

"This is going to be random, but you're probably the best boyfriend I have ever had." I had no idea why I'd said it but maybe I was feeling sentimental over him bringing me here.

The cone that Nash was about to consume stopped midway to his mouth. "What do you mean probably?"

I couldn't help but giggle. "Okay, fine. You're the best boyfriend I've ever had."

Nash used his shoulder to nudge me, and I giggled again.

"This time next year, we'll be entering our freshmen year at Brentson University."

"That was random, and you mean if I get in." I'd done my best to keep my insecurity about this to myself, but it slipped out this time. Nash was, without a doubt, getting in. Even if he hadn't gotten as good of grades as he had, he would probably still get into Brentson based on his last name alone.

I, on the other hand, didn't have that leverage. While I, too, had good grades, I would also be relying on scholarships and student loans to make my dream to go to Brentson a reality. My mom and I were already discussing how we would make it work if I were to get in, and I was doing everything in my power to not place another burden on her shoulders. Even though we were fortunate that our house was paid off, Mom was already working two jobs to help us make ends meet as it was.

I knew going to Brentson would open so many doors for me and my career. I knew that when the time came, I would be able to help my mom so she didn't have to work as much, if she didn't want to. It also meant that Nash and I could stay together and not have to worry about a long-distance relationship.

Nash reached over and pulled my chair closer to his and slung his arm around my shoulders. "You're getting in, I don't understand why you keep doubting yourself. You're one of the smartest people I know, and Brentson University would benefit so much from having you."

Nash's words almost made me want to cry. But instead, I focused on eating the ice cream cone in my hand. When I finished swallowing some more ice cream, I said, "You don't have to say that just because you're my boyfriend."

"I'm not. I truly meant every word, and you need to believe in yourself more. It's easier said than done and..."

This time, my smile returned because he was right. I needed to have more faith in myself. Even with my insecurities about the future, I was excited about what this year would bring as we wrapped up our high school years, and I knew that with Nash by my side this year, there's no way that this wouldn't be one of the best years of my life.

I FELT MYSELF WAKING UP, and I was irritated. Being caught up in my dream of the past was a safe space for me. Although I knew it was a dream, it was almost exactly how I recalled the date happening in real life. Like your stereotypical teenager, I was having a hard time dealing with my insecurities back then, but I still longed to be transported back in time to that happier moment.

It was a time where my life felt like it was spinning out of control because of all of the big decisions I had to make. Little did I know that I would be picking out a casket and making funeral arrangements less than a year later. And my life has been hectic ever since. Returning to reality for me meant that I was back to the shitstorm that I was living in.

I was in no way referencing the cabin where I was being kept. It was nice and cozy from the little I'd seen of it. No, I was referring to the man who had enough nerve to kidnap me and bring me here.

I opened my eyes and noticed that it was still daylight. Either I'd only slept a few hours, or I'd slept through the night and into the next day. At this point, it felt like either option was possible.

When I tried to get out of bed this time, signs of my nausea didn't appear. A huge sigh of relief passed through my lips just before my stomach growled. That made sense, given that I didn't know how long it had been since I'd last eaten and whatever I had eaten was now down the toilet.

It was then that I realized the urge to use the bathroom was what woke me up. My breathing also wasn't in the best state. I crossed my fingers as I removed the comforter, and it was then that I noticed some scratches and bruises on my arm. Guess that happens when you throw yourself out of a moving car. I walked to the bathroom hoping that I wouldn't get nauseous again and that I would find a toothbrush and toothpaste in there. I must have had a bit of luck on my side because I found a still-wrapped toothbrush and what looked to be a brand-new tube of toothpaste waiting for me.

I used the bathroom and made quick work of brushing my teeth before I threw some water on my face. The drowsiness that I experienced the last time I was awake was still there but not nearly as bad as it had been. After washing up, I felt more refreshed and while a shower would do wonders, I was a little concerned about fainting while taking one.

As I was drying my face, I finally got the courage to look into the mirror, and what I saw made me gasp. I looked rough, to say the least. It was as if I'd been dragged through the mud and back again several times. My skin looked paler than normal and the bags under my eyes made it appear as if I hadn't slept in weeks, even though I had just gotten plenty of sleep, or so I thought. At least my face made out much better than the rest of my body in terms of scrapes and bruises.

I sighed. Eventually, all of this would heal anyway.

Strangely enough, I found one of my old hair ties on the counter and threw my hair into a quick ponytail. Had I put it there when I was awake last just before I started throwing up? I couldn't remember and it didn't really matter anyway.

I tried my best to look as presentable as possible while also knowing this was the best I was going to look. There was nothing else I could do to fix this. I pushed my shoulders back and walked from the bathroom through the bedroom and to the other door in the room. If it didn't lead me into the living area, I'd be shocked.

I gave myself a small pep talk as I tried to summon the small amount of energy I had left. I took a deep breath to steady myself before I opened the bedroom door because I didn't know what waited for me on the other side of it.

As I opened the bedroom door, I was surprised by what I found. Whoever designed this place made sure to keep the warm and cozy feel throughout the home, which also stunned me. With someone like Nash Henson having access to it, I was expecting things to look more extravagant. This isn't to say that the cabin looked horrible, it actually looked very nice, but it made me wonder how Nash was able to stay in this place. It didn't look anything like the other properties I knew the Henson family owned, including both Nash's apartment in Brentson and his parents' apartment in the city.

I became distracted because my nose was met with what could only be described as pure heaven. I was having a hard time placing exactly what was cooking but it smelled amazing.

"You're awake." I turned and found Nash standing near the stove.

"Yes, yes, I am. And since we are stating the obvious, I want to go."

"Are you hungry?"

My stomach chose this moment to growl. "Looks like that is a yes."

"I figured as much since you haven't eaten."

"Don't change the subject. We still haven't addressed when you are taking me home."

"I thought that was obvious. No can do, Little Bird. We are staying here for a while."

I thought my body only began to shake due to a lack of food, but this conversation was also a contributing factor. Too bad this discussion needed to happen now. The sooner I was out of here, the better. "There is nothing stopping you from taking me back to campus. I won't tell anyone that this happened."

"Once again, no can do." Nash looked over his shoulder at me. "I'm cooking lasagna in the oven. Would you like a piece? If not, I can whip up some soup or something else."

I could feel my emotions were tittering on the edge of spilling over. I tried to hold back the tears that threatened to fall. Crying wasn't a common occurrence for me, but it seemed to be happening more frequently now and I couldn't blame myself.

I took a deep breath in as I tried to prevent the inevitable. "Why won't you let me go? Based on what it looks like from here, there's nothing stopping me from running out that door right now."

"No, but every time you run, I'm going to find you."

My eyes widened at his comment, and it didn't go unnoticed by me that he hadn't completely answered my question. As I opened my mouth to speak, he spoke again.

"You're safer here with me."

Something inside me snapped. There was no way he could be serious. "What do you mean I'm safer here with you. I watched you kill someone, and you almost killed me!"

"I didn't almost kill you, but you should keep that in mind next time you try to piss me off."

"Was that a threat?"

"No. It was a promise. Would you like a piece of lasagna or not?"

I'd be a fool not to take it. It did smell good, and I needed to eat. But I also didn't trust Nash at all.

"I'll have a piece as long as you take a bite of mine and eat it first."

He raised an eyebrow at my demand. "Seriously? What the hell is wrong with you?"

"What do you mean what the hell is wrong with me? You're the one murdering and kidnapping people and *you* think something is wrong with me?"

The dangerous look in his eyes scared the shit out of me because I thought it might be a hint of what was to come. "Goodwin, we're going to sit down and have a relaxing early dinner before you pass out and then I have to deal with that."

Nash walked away from the stove, grabbed my hand, and almost dragged me to the dining room table. He forced me down into the seat before walking back into the kitchen. While he was distracted with the food, I scanned the room for possible ways that I could escape when the time came. There were a few windows and the front door, all of which might be good opportunities for me to get the hell out of here.

Were there any weapons in here that I could use to my advantage? There had to be something that I hadn't had an opportunity to discover yet.

The tears in my eyes seemed to vanish as I threw myself into the mindset of finding a weapon and trying to plan my escape. My attention was brought back to Nash as I found him walking out of the kitchen with a dish in each hand. When he put one in front of me, I had to admit it looked as delicious as it smelled. My mouth salivated at the sight, but that didn't mean it was edible.

Nash placed his dish in front of the seat next to mine before walking back into the kitchen. I assumed he was getting our drinks, but I didn't waste any more time trying to figure out what he was doing.

All of my attention was drawn to finding a way out of here as fast as possible.

5

RAVEN

I patted my thigh, and for the first time since I'd gotten here, I realized I didn't have my phone. When I ran from Nash's car, I'd made sure to grab it, with the plan to call someone as soon as I got far enough away from him. Of course that plan had failed miserably, and now I was willing to bet he took it so I couldn't reach out to anyone for help.

As if he knew I was thinking about him, Nash came out of the kitchen too fast and barely gave me a second to think let alone act. It hurt my soul that I was stuck here for the time being.

When he reached the table again, he put a glass of water in front of me and a beer down for himself.

"You didn't even bother to ask me if I wanted something else to drink," I said.

"You're more than likely dehydrated, and water is one of the better fixes for that."

I knew that he was right, but that didn't mean I would just

give in. He did kidnap me, and he was keeping me here against my will. I certainly wasn't feeling agreeable. "That doesn't mean that you shouldn't have asked me what I wanted."

"I didn't feel the need."

His words and the look in his eyes sent even more red flags through my mind. Fear tore through me like a tornado because I truly had no idea what he was capable of.

"This is all so fucked up," I mumbled under my breath. I looked up to make sure he didn't have a reaction to what I'd said. When he hadn't, I calmed down slightly.

My lip trembled before I could stop it. I hated that his words were having this effect on me. His demeaning attitude toward me made me feel like shit, but I needed to remain calm. I'd seen what he was capable of, and I needed to make sure that I didn't end up in the same situation as the guy who tried to kidnap me.

I watched as Nash took a seat next to me when I assumed that he would want the seat across the table from me. I decided that taking a sip of water was probably the safest bet since I'd heard him get the water from the tap on the fridge, so I grabbed the glass and brought it to my lips. Although I knew it would be refreshing, I hated that he was right.

Nash grabbed his fork and leaned over and took a piece of the lasagna on my plate and brought it to his lips. The look in his eyes was slightly playful as he put the fork in his mouth and licked it clean. He stared me down as he chewed his food, to prove he hadn't poisoned it. If he was trying to make me feel foolish, he'd failed. One could never be too sure after what I'd experienced over the last twenty-four to forty-eight hours.

I picked up my fork too and used it to break off a piece of the lasagna before sticking it into my mouth. It tasted like a delicious explosion. Before I could stop myself, I moaned, and I immediately regretted drawing more attention to myself. Nash looked at me with an eyebrow raised. I stared at him, daring him to say something. When he didn't, I looked back down at the food in front of me and the next thing I knew, I was shoving another piece of food into my mouth followed by another. It was as if I hadn't eaten in days and needed to get as much food into my stomach as quickly as possible.

Speaking of which, I didn't know what day it actually was. I held my question until I ate a few more mouthfuls, and when I finally felt as if I wasn't going to pass out any longer, I took another sip of water. The liquid soothed my dry, parched throat.

"What's today?" I blurted out the question without giving it a second thought. I was irritated at having to ask him at all.

"Friday."

I was supposed to meet Nash on Thursday night which meant that I didn't sleep an entire day away. That tiny bit was reassuring to me in this huge sea of mess.

Then again, I also could have slept for a week straight and have been none the wiser.

"Yesterday was when you killed—"

"Watch it."

I swallowed hard. "Yesterday was when I was at Chevalier Manor?"

"That is correct."

His tone told me that proceeding with this same line of questioning would land me deeper into a hole that I wouldn't be able to climb out of. So, I changed the subject. "Shouldn't you be preparing for your football game right now?"

"Maybe. Maybe not." He didn't elaborate any further, and I told myself if he continued this way, I couldn't be liable for my actions.

My changing the subject eased tensions slightly between us, but my irritation was increasing. I was tired of dancing around the real reason I was talking to him because if I had the choice, I'd ignore him for the rest of eternity. I put my fork down and said, "I deserve to know why you won't take me back to campus."

"Because you're not safe there."

"And I'm safe here with you?" I was itching to slap him in the face, but I grabbed my glass of water to give my hand something else to do.

Nash scoffed. "It's the only choice you have at the moment, sweetheart."

I rolled my eyes at the condescending way, he said "sweetheart". "And why is that?"

"Because we don't know if the asshole who tried to kidnap you had any friends." He drank from his beer bottle.

"So, I'm safer with you? You drugged me, asshole." My grip tightened on the glass. I debated throwing it but all that would do is further heighten the animosity between us.

Nash shrugged. "I had to make sure I got you here as quickly as possible, and I knew there was no way you weren't going to fight back. I did what I had to do."

"That's illegal."

Nash shrugged. "Wouldn't be the first time I did something that was."

Touché. He did make a great point.

"And nothing in your mind is telling you how dangerous this entire idea of yours is? Hell, you kidnapped me and are holding me against my will, not to mention you murdered someone else. If the police find out—"

Nash looked at me over the top of his beer bottle. "The police will never find out because whatever you think you saw is dead and buried. Since you think you were drugged, your recollection of things might be a little... fuzzy."

"Don't attempt to gaslight me. I know what I saw. I watched you kill that man."

"In reference to the kidnapping claim, you're free to go, Goodwin. If you wanted to walk out the door right now, there are no special locks or restraints holding you back. But I'm warning you, if you attempt to leave, I will fucking hunt you down. Each and every time."

I believed every word he said. His words made me feel something I didn't want to feel. I was outraged, but in some kind of fucked-up way, it was as if his words had caressed my cheek, preparing me for what his next move might be if I did manage to escape. I was frightened, but the look in his eyes also excited me. What the hell was wrong with me?

I shook my head to rid myself of thoughts of what it might look like if he did indeed catch me. I couldn't let that cloud my judgment, because I knew I needed to get out of here. But there was no way I was going to manage to create a plan and execute it now. No, I needed more time so I did the only thing I could do right now: survive.

I focused on eating again. It was what my body and soul needed. Whoever made this food had made sure that it was delicious. It helped to refuel me, and I was starting to feel more alive again. Trying to think was no longer such a struggle, and the drowsiness I'd been feeling was going away.

I wiped my lips with a napkin and asked, "Can I have my phone?"

"Why? So, you can call someone?"

"I want it—" Why was I pleading with him? This felt asinine because it was my phone.

"No."

"Give me my phone."

"No."

"At the very least, I need to let Izzy know that I am all right. I don't want her to worry."

"You're going to tell her everything that happened. She's under the impression that you're sick and can't talk right now, but maybe if you're a good girl, I'll let you call her in a couple of days."

His comments left me stunned. The only thing I could manage to do was blink at him for several seconds. "If I'm a good girl?"

Nash smirked at me but said nothing.

I needed to fill the silence because I couldn't take it. "Izzy thinks I'm what?"

"You're very sick. It was the best way to explain why you were absent to...well, everyone. You'll be able to do your work from here once you're feeling up to it. You can think of this as a staycation."

"The audacity that you have is out of this fucking world." I shook my head as I tried to process all that he'd just told me. Then another idea popped into my mind. "Then what is your excuse for also not being able to attend classes, football practice, or whatever the hell else it is that you do?"

This time he grinned at me and looked me dead in the eye. "We've recently reunited, Little Bird. I'm your loving, caring boyfriend who is going out of his way to tend to your *every* need."

6

RAVEN

"We're what? You're doing what? There's no way anyone is going to believe that shit."

Nash sat back into his chair and folded his arms across his chest with a grin that I used to think was one of the sexiest things in this world. "You'd be surprised how many people fell for the idea that you and I had gotten back together. They completely bought that now I was being the loving supporting boyfriend, who was nursing you back to health. It's pretty genius actually, if I do say so myself."

Although I hated that he lied to who knows who, part of me wished that one-half of his comment was true. I wished he was back to being the kind, caring boyfriend that I remembered from high school. Instead, I was sitting next to a monster who had no problem doing whatever it took to get whatever he wanted.

"And this goes without saying, but everything between us remains the same," he said, interrupting the spiraling rabbit hole I was about to fall into. "Our little game still remains in exchange for me not telling your secret and—"

This time, I cut him off. "The secret you think you know is a lie. Van Henson is full of shit and deep down you know it because you know him better than most people. Since the secret you think you know is a damn lie, your little game is over, and you can kiss my whole ass."

"But I've already done that, Little Bird." He was obviously referring to our sexcapades, and the heated look on his face suggested that he might have been replaying one of the adventures in his mind.

I couldn't help but roll my eyes as I resisted the urge to punch him in the face. It was followed by me throwing my hands up in disgust. There was no way that this battle was over, I just needed more time to think and prepare. I pushed my chair back, suddenly losing the rest of my appetite. I stood up and left the dining room table.

The polite thing to do would have been to bring my dishes back into the kitchen but I couldn't give a shit about being polite under these circumstances. This was probably one of the worst dinners I had ever had, and it had nothing to do with the lovely food I had just eaten. I reached the bedroom door and just as I was about to walk through it, there was a knock on the cabin's front door.

My body froze. Was this my chance to escape? Had someone come here to save me?

I slowly turned around and took a step into the bedroom, in case I needed to make a run for it. There was at least one window here that I might be able to get out of pretty quickly, but it being closed would slow me down. I held my breath as I watched Nash walk toward the front door. Nothing about him gave off the impression that he was nervous. He didn't seem surprised by the knocking. I waited with bated breath for him to open the door. When he finally did, my eyes widened. I studied the man standing in front of Nash as I tried to place where I'd seen him before. Was he the guy I saw Nash walking with when I first arrived in Brentson? Before I could confirm, I became distracted by a petite blonde standing next to him that I easily recognized.

"Bianca? What the fuck are you doing here?" Nash asked the question before I did. That he was surprised to see her here gave me a glimmer of hope. If she wasn't a part of his plan, maybe she could help me escape.

"I wanted to talk to you, so I went to your apartment. I was there to ask you about what happened with Mom and Dad after the party at our house, but you weren't home. Then this asshole walked through the door and told me that he was going to see you, so I made him bring me along. He wouldn't tell me where we were going, but I pieced it together once I recognized the roads we were taking."

Bianca stopped talking and suddenly her eyes settled on me. They then drifted between Nash and me as she tried to put together this mystery that was unfolding in front of her. She walked over to me and gave me a small hug before returning to stand near her brother. We hadn't been incredibly close when Nash and I dated in high school, due to us being older than her, but she was always kind to me when I saw her.

"It makes sense why Nash is here because we co-own this place, but why are you? And what happened to you? There's so many scratches and bruises... I'm being rude and I apologize for being offensive," she said while looking at me.

Before Nash or I could speak or move, the man with Bianca pushed his way into the cabin, which seemed to be growing smaller by the second with the amount of people that were in it. He placed a large black duffel bag at Nash's feet before taking a step back.

"Next time, give me a warning if I'm going to have to babysit your sister for a couple of hours."

Bianca turned and glared at him.

He took a step toward me and introduced himself.

"By the way, I'm Easton, this fucker's best friend."

"Nice to meet you. My name is Raven." I didn't bother putting a label on my relationship with Nash because, honestly, what would I use? His ex? His fuck buddy? His captive? Any one of those could apply.

We shook hands before taking a step back from one another.

Bianca cleared her throat, drawing our eyes back to her as she refocused her attention on us. She side-eyed Easton before she turned to me and repeated her question again.

"I'm here because your brother—"

"Wants to keep you safe," Nash said, finishing my sentence and changing the ending I would have given.

I glared at him because I didn't appreciate him answering for me and telling a lie. "I can speak for myself, thank you very much."

I still wasn't convinced that he was trying to keep me safe versus finding another avenue that he could use to control me. It pained me that both options were potentially valid. What caught me slightly off guard was that Nash had told the truth this time. Instead of feeding them the narrative that I was sick, he'd let Bianca and Easton in on his little dark secret. He could have easily planned it so that I wouldn't have been around when they came by, but he hadn't.

Bianca's mouth dropped open and Easton studied Nash, I assumed trying to figure out if he was telling the truth or not. I didn't blame either of them one bit.

"Safe from what?" Bianca questioned.

"Last night, Raven was almost kidnapped," Nash responded while giving me a look of warning.

"What do you mean almost kidnapped?" Easton said.

"Raven was almost kidnapped, but I stopped it from happening." Nash didn't elaborate anymore. I wondered if he would mention that he murdered the guy, but so far, we were the only two people in the room who knew that he'd done that.

"And why aren't we going to the police about this?"

I had to fight the urge to clap. Bianca was asking the right questions, in my opinion.

"It's complicated and would only cause more confusion if the police were brought in. So we are staying here until further notice." Nash glanced at Easton and said, "Were you able to find everything I asked for?"

"I was."

"Perfect. Would you both like to stay for dinner?"

The look on my face must have been comical because Bianca smiled. Her eyes darted between Nash and me and then she said, "I would love to."

"Well, the princess has spoken, so it looks like we will be staying."

Bianca turned and glared at Easton once more. I couldn't help but wonder what was going on between them. It briefly removed the stress I'd been feeling because I could refocus it on them, and I had to admit that I was mildly entertained.

We, once again, sat back down at the dining room table.

Nash went into the kitchen to get pieces of lasagna for his sister and best friend.

An idea popped into my head. "Bianca, can we move Nash's stuff to the other end of the table so that you and I can chat? It's been so long since we've talked."

It wasn't a lie. I did want to catch up with her, and if this was a way I could put distance between Nash and me, then I was going to take it. Bianca raised an eyebrow at me as Easton did as I asked. She sat down in the chair that was once occupied by Nash, and I gave her a genuine smile. I couldn't wait to see his reaction.

When Nash walked back into the dining room, he noticed the change in seating arrangements immediately. He gave me a small nod, acknowledging that I was the mastermind behind the switch. I couldn't help but feel a small amount of glee because it felt as if I'd won this round.

Nash placed a plate in front of Easton and then said, "I have one more favor to ask."

"What's that? And thanks, man."

Nash nodded. "I want to borrow your SUV while we're here."

Easton's eyes nearly popped out of his skull. "You want to do what?"

"To ease the burden for you, I'll let you have the Jag until I'm back on campus."

Easton thought about it for a split second before he said, "Hell yes!"

"Well, since that is taken care of, let's eat."

I hadn't finished eating my meal, but I no longer had an appetite. Instead, I sat there and used my fork to push my food around my plate, just to give me something to do. The one thing I found beneficial about having Bianca and Easton see me was that they could confirm my whereabouts in case something did happen. Then again, the likelihood that they would turn on Nash was low so it might have been pointless after all.

"I'm done eating so I'm going to put my dishes in the sink. Can I take anything else?"

Everyone at the table shook their heads so I picked up my glass and plate and walked into the kitchen. As I was walking to the sink, I spotted Nash's cellphone sitting there on the counter. I placed the dishes in the sink and looked over my shoulder. No one seemed to be paying attention to me, so I reached over and grabbed his phone.

When I clicked the screen, it immediately lit up and brought me to the text message conversation that he had with Easton. A quick skim told me that he'd planned this whole thing out with him, where Easton ended up picking up some things for Nash and some things for me from our respective houses and brought them here.

I moved on and found his contacts. I knew, at least at one point, he had Izzy's number in his phone, and if I could just dial her and give her a hint as to what was going on, I might have a chance to—

The phone flew out of my hands, and I found Nash standing next to me with a hard glare. I'd been so focused on the phone that I hadn't heard him sneak up on me.

"Remember what I said, Little Bird."

"Everything all right in there?" Easton called out from the dining room area. I guess our commotion had been louder than I thought.

Nash gave me a wolfish grin, before he said, "Everything is perfect. Shall we?"

I stared down as he held out his arm for me to grab like we were at a fancy event, and he was about to escort me in. I pushed his arm out of the way and walked back into the dining room area and took my seat.

There had to be something I could do to tell Bianca that her brother was full of shit and that I needed to get out of here. I figured she might be the easier of the two to convince because, although she and Nash were siblings, she and I at least knew each other, unlike Easton, who I just officially met tonight.

I tried to catch her eye while she and Easton ate dinner and without Nash knowing, but I failed. The three of them seemed to have a friendly conversation, but I felt like an outsider to the whole thing. Not that I wanted to participate in it, anyway.

"Is there anything I can do to help?"

Bianca's question brought me out of the daze I'd put myself in after my attempts at getting her attention didn't work. This was my chance.

"Could you take me back to campus?"

Bianca tilted her head and out of the corner of my eye, I watched as Nash shifted in his seat. Without looking at him, I could tell that it wasn't out of nervousness about where this conversation might lead. It was out of anger. I could feel his gaze on me, lighting a fire within me in more ways than one.

"If there's someone trying to kidnap you, it would make sense for you to stay somewhere where no one would expect to find you."

She had a good point, but the biggest problem with this

whole scenario was that it left me with Nash, who I now knew had no issue with murdering someone. Where did that leave me?

"I don't feel comfortable being here." I silently begged her with my eyes to agree with me.

"It would be no issue to take you back on my end," Easton chimed in. Maybe it should have been him that I was trying to convince, not Bianca.

"Raven will be safer here and I don't want to put anyone on campus at risk if the kidnapper comes back and tries to finish what he started. We wouldn't want any of her room-mates getting hurt because we acted too hastily. We've both been excused from campus for the time being, so I think it's wise if we stay here."

Nash knew just where to hit and made the perfect case for why I should remain here for the time being. Of course I didn't want anyone getting hurt because of me. I couldn't help but wonder if his words were also intended as a threat.

I turned my head and looked at Nash. He had a look of triumph on his face. He'd known that he had me cornered. This felt worse than when he'd found me in the library and dragged me into the stairwell to issue his original threat when he was still trying to force me to leave Brentson. I had no choice but to agree with his stance, and I nodded my head slowly before looking down at my hands.

My nervousness increased as I waited for Easton and Bianca to finish their meal. I'd taken a risk by asking to be taken back to campus. I'd failed and now I would have to face my consequences.

When Bianca and Easton finished eating, Easton said,

"We should head back. Some of us are playing football tomorrow and should rest up."

Nash shook his head and said, "Fine. Don't worry about the dishes, I'll grab them after I walk you two to the door."

My heart sank further into my body. He wasn't going to give me the opportunity to be alone with either of them so that I could try to convince them one last time that I didn't belong here. Everyone but me stood up and started moving toward the door. I hesitated another moment and then I stood up too.

Bianca turned to me and said, "If you need anything, either one of you can text me and I'll try my best to help. I have no issue driving out here to do it."

"Same here, but I'd prefer if it was without you, though."

"Enough," Nash said, ending Bianca and Easton's argument before it could really begin. "I'm sure we'll be fine, but we'll keep you updated."

When Nash shut the front door, I could have cried. As soon as the door was locked, Nash turned, and his long legs quickly ate the distance between him and me. He grabbed me by the arm and while it wasn't painful, I was still frightened because I didn't know what he would do next. I knew I couldn't show him that fear though. It would only antagonize him further. I pulled to remove my arm from his grip, but he wouldn't budge.

"Get off of me."

"Fighting me is useless. I'll let you go when I'm ready to let you go. Figuratively and literally."

He leaned down and my eyes widened. The look in his eyes was wild and it brought me back to the glee I'd seen on his face when he'd killed Paul. The smile that crept onto his face made me tremble and there was no doubt in my mind that he'd felt it.

Nash's lips were a whisper away from mine and then he said, "Try that stunt again, and I'll have no problem hand-cuffing you to that bed in there and spanking that ass of yours until you can barely walk."

7

RAVEN

"We're headed out in five minutes."

The sound of Nash's voice made me jump and place my hand on my chest. I tossed the book I'd been reading on the floor and looked at him. "Are we going back to campus?"

"No. Throw on whatever you need to put on and then we'll be ready to go." He turned and left the room before I could get a chance to inquire further.

It was the next evening after our dinner with Easton and Bianca. I thought about telling him no, that I wasn't leaving the cabin under these circumstances, but this might be my only chance at getting out of here. I needed to hope that he was taking me somewhere and not trying to murder me in the woods or something else along those lines.

For the most part, Nash had left me alone and I stayed in the bedroom. I tried to make sure that I was out of his way, and I'd succeeded up until now. This was an opportunity I wasn't about to let slip away.

I bent down to pick up the book and placed it on the red

velvet chair opposite me. I found a sweatshirt and jeans and tossed them on without a second thought. This was the most motivated I'd felt since I'd arrived here.

Nash didn't say a word when he saw that I'd walked out of the bedroom, and I followed him to the SUV in silence. He started the vehicle and drove up the unpaved road.

"Where are we going?"

"To a store to pick up a few things."

So we were going to be out in public. Excellent.

The ride was quiet, and I couldn't have asked for anything else. I rubbed my hands against my face as I waited for Nash to pull into a parking spot. It was weird seeing Nash drive this vehicle instead of his sports car, but if someone wanted to keep a low profile, this was the way to do it. The larger space was a small consolation for me; at least I could stay a little further away from him in the SUV.

I didn't know why Nash decided this was the perfect time to do a quick store run for essentials anyway. If he was truly worried about my "safety," staying in the cabin seemed a wiser choice. Perhaps he was doing this to show me that he didn't have any fears about me trying to escape.

I debated with myself about whether it would be worth trying to run and get help from someone in the store while we were here, but I didn't know how far the Henson name reached or if their political influence was powerful enough to get this all conveniently swept under the rug. I did know that he wasn't likely to let me out of his sight while we were out.

"Grab whatever you need while we are in there. Cost doesn't matter as far as I'm concerned."

"Anything?"

"Anything."

He couldn't be serious. "I need quite a bit of clothes since Easton didn't bring any with him."

"Then grab them." His impatience with me was clearly evident in his tone.

He ended our discussion by opening his car door and stepping outside. I rolled my eyes and followed suit.

I noticed he didn't even spare a glance at me opening my own door. A pang of sadness hit me unexpectedly, but I knew exactly where it came from. This was such a stark contrast to how he'd acted in high school, and whenever I was slapped with a reminder about how much things had changed, it hurt.

Nash grabbed a cart and together we walked up and down the aisles of the store. I had no problem with grabbing the things I thought I would need for a few days away from my home, even though I had no intention of staying with him. I knew I needed to do something to get myself out of this mess and being here might be the perfect opportunity. The longer we spent walking around the store, the more time I had to look for an opportunity to get away from Nash.

I debated causing a commotion while Nash pushed our cart, which was now almost filled to the brim, but the cashier's wide-eyed look made me pause. The nametag on his shirt said his name was Todd.

"Nash Henson. I wasn't expecting you to walk into my store this evening."

Todd nodded at me before turning his attention back to Nash. I didn't feel the least bit slighted as I took a step away from Nash. "Are you staying up this way for a while? We missed you at the game today."

"Yeah, it sucked not to play, but I'll be back on the field

soon." Nash gave him his charming grin that always had everyone falling to their knees within seconds.

I held back the scream that I wanted to let loose. In hindsight, it was a good thing I hadn't caused a big scene that would have left this town's football hero being called into question. They would have for sure buried me to save him so he could bring another national championship to the region.

When Todd finished ringing us up, I balked at the total, but Nash just handed over his credit card without a second thought. We both said goodbye to Todd, and I followed behind Nash as we started to make our way to the exit. We were stopped by Todd calling Nash's name.

"Can you autograph a couple of things for me?"

Nash looked at me before giving Todd a tight smile. "Of course."

"Wow, I can't wait to tell Bob about this," Todd mumbled under his breath but loud enough for all three of us to hear.

I crossed my arms and slowly walked away from Nash while he was distracted. I'd never seen someone sign things so quickly before in my life, and as soon as I got near the exit, Nash was right there, glaring at me as if he knew what I'd been planning to do.

It had been disturbing to watch how nice he'd been to Todd, giving him every bit of his charming personality, before the complete one-eighty he'd done when it came to me. He was, without a doubt, one way to the public and another way in private.

I looked down as Nash waved goodbye to Todd and the two of us walked out to Easton's SUV, where Nash loaded all of the things we bought while I sat in the passenger seat.

I fought back a yawn as he entered the vehicle and was

relieved when we finally pulled off and were on our way back to the cabin. That relief was short-lived, though, because then I would have to deal with Nash for the rest of the night.

"That wasn't so bad, was it? Outside of you trying to escape?"

"No, I guess it wasn't."

"There was a reason I chose to come here so late at night."

Nash didn't elaborate, but I didn't need him to because I quickly pieced together what he meant. He'd intentionally chosen to come here this late to decrease the chances of me being able to go for help. But I guess I could thank my lucky stars that he didn't keep me locked up in the cabin while he did this outing alone.

I didn't bother looking at Nash because my emotions and thoughts were currently all over the place. I was stuck between thinking I'd just missed an opportunity to go back to Brentson and being grateful that no one had come up and tried to attack me. All I wanted to do was to go back home and get ready for bed. Instead, I was being driven to a cabin I didn't want to go to, and now that the chloroform was fully out of my system, I didn't know how much sleep I would get because I was worried about what Nash might be doing.

We stayed in silence for the rest of the drive. As soon as Nash pulled to a complete stop in front of the cabin, I was out the door, because I didn't want to deal with being that close in proximity to Nash anymore.

After we brought everything into the house, I immediately grabbed the things I would need for a shower. The one I'd taken this morning was fine, but with some of the items that I normally loved using, it would make my shower better. I took my time and when I was done, I put on my new long-sleeved pajamas and let my hair hang loose. When I was dressed, I walked into the living area, where I found Nash lounging on the couch. I didn't spare him another glance, but I could feel him watching every move I made.

I walked into the kitchen and searched for a glass. Once I found one, I poured water into it and took a long gulp before refilling it. When I was satisfied with how much water I'd had, I glanced at the kitchen counter and found the keys to Easton's SUV. I quickly grabbed them without thinking about it and walked through the kitchen into the living room. Nash hadn't moved from the couch, so I continued on my way into the bedroom.

I'd taken another sip from my glass of water before placing it on the bedside table. I was about to get underneath the covers with the keys still in my hand when Nash came into the room.

"What are you doing in here?" I took a step back and moved my hand that still clutched the keys behind my back.

Nash looked at me before he removed his shirt. "What does it look like I'm doing? Going to bed."

I stared at his chest for way too long before I thought up a response. "No, you're not. You can sleep out in the living room like you have been."

He scoffed. "I'm not sleeping in the living room again."

Him sleeping in the living room had been amazing because it gave me a chance to breathe. It had been my saving grace. I didn't want to be liable for suffocating him with a pillow while he was asleep during the middle of the night. "There's no way you're sleeping in here with me. I'll go sleep on the couch."

"Are you scared to sleep next to me, Little Bird? It's not like you haven't done it before."

He took a step toward me, resulting in me taking a step back to keep the distance between us the same.

"I'm not afraid of you." That was a lie, but I went with it. "When we slept in the same bed together, it was before you decided that it was a great idea to hold me captive. If I thought I despised you after you cornered me in the library, it doesn't compare to how I feel now. You make me fucking sick."

He took another step toward me. "That's not what you were saying—"

"Stay away from me." I took a step back toward the nightstand. I really needed to get him out of here before he realized I had the keys to Easton's SUV.

"Goodwin—"

I rolled my eyes. "We're back to that shit again."

"There's no harm in us sleeping in the same bed."

"There's plenty of harm in it, and I don't want to be near you. That should be enough."

Nash's eyes studied me, but he kept his emotions behind a mask.

"Your mouth is saying one thing, but your body is telling me something completely different." He took another step toward me.

There was nowhere for me to go, and it would take him three steps max to grab me. "I said, get away from me!"

It was as if Nash took my demand as a challenge. As he took another step, the world felt as if it was closing in on me, and suddenly, I began to feel claustrophobic. All of my senses were yelling at me to get out of this situation as fast as possible. He took another step toward me, and I reacted.

I grabbed the glass of water that I placed on the bedside table and threw it at him. My aim was wildly off, but it served as a distraction. Nash ducked and covered his head. When he looked up at me from his place on the floor, his wide eyes and slightly opened mouth all showed that he didn't believe what I'd just done. This was my chance. I took it as an opportunity to run.

I managed to dart around him without him being able to grab at my feet, and I sprinted from the room as fast as I could. I didn't stop to think, let alone put on shoes, before I yanked the door open. Before I could run outside, Nash threw an arm around my torso, but I elbowed him, causing him to slightly break his hold, and then I kicked back. I didn't take the time to look at where my hits landed because my focus was on getting to the vehicle outside.

He cursed and let me go, giving me the opportunity to run again. For a haphazard plan that I'd put no thought into, it was going decently well, if only I could make it into the vehicle and lock the door before Nash got to me.

It felt like déjà vu as I unlocked the door from the house and ran the short distance to the car. Just as I was about to close the driver's side door, Nash appeared and stopped it.

"The longer you take to get out of this fucking car, Little Bird, the angrier I'm going to become."

"Let me go, Nash!"

"I already warned you."

I tried to twist my body so I could kick him again, but he must have recognized what I was planning. He quickly moved his body to block my attempt at pulling the door closed and yanked me out of the car. Once he had a firm hold around my stomach, he closed the door with his other hand.

I struggled against his hold and yelled for help as he dragged me back into the cabin. He didn't say a word as I fought to try to get him to release his grip on me. If I could just get loose, I would have another shot at making it to the door.

But Nash was too strong. Even attempts to kick him in places that I knew would cause the most damage were futile. He brought me through the living room and didn't stop until he walked into the bedroom and threw me down on the bed.

Before I could blink, he was climbing on top of me and held my hands above my head as he stared down into my eyes.

"I promised you that every time you ran, I would hunt you down and bring you back to me. You're mine, Little Bird. Now it's time to show you just what happens when you make me chase after you."

8

NASH

Raven's ability to infuriate me never ceased to amaze me. I thought it was comical that she tried to pull a stunt while we were at the store. Her decision to try and steal Easton's SUV had done nothing but piss me off. Now it was time to take out all my pent-up aggression on her body.

At first, I thought that her heavy breathing was a result of how hard she'd tried to get away from me, but the dilation of her eyes told me otherwise. My gaze danced over her chest, and I could see the hardness of her nipples through the shirt she had on. I turned to focus on her lips and imagined what it would feel like to have them wrapped around my cock. The image of her down on her knees with me fucking her mouth made me even harder. When she ran the tip of her tongue across her bottom lip, I was a goner. She wanted this just as much as I did.

With my hands still holding onto her wrists, I leaned down and planted a rough kiss on her lips. It felt raw and needy. I was demanding all of her and I would take nothing less. She resisted at first, trying to pull away, before giving up and kissing me back, forcing a low groan from my mouth. I wanted to devour every inch of her, but first we would start here.

Deep down I knew as soon as I caught her that this would be anything but slow. The need to consume her, all of her, was just so intense and it was a feeling I refused to ignore. It felt as if it had been so long since we'd been together, and I didn't want to waste another millisecond before I got to be inside of her.

I broke our kiss and ran my finger along her lips, mesmerized by the sight before me. She hadn't been back in my life for long, but she'd turned me into a walking contradiction. I both wanted to get revenge for the pain she'd caused me, and I also wanted to make her happy. The conflicting feelings I'd had for her increased the desire to punish her for what she'd done.

I wrapped my hand around her throat, not enough to choke her, but firm enough that I could feel her swallow hard. I smiled to myself when her body trembled under my touch. Having her like this was intoxicating, something that I could easily become addicted to. When she sighed, I fought back a smile. She was enjoying this just as much as I was. Despite our differences, we'd always been electrifying in bed, and I knew that this time would be no different.

I loosened my grip before I moved my hand lower until I touched her breasts through the shirt she had on. Instead of immediately making a move to lift the barrier between her skin and my hand, I played with her nipples through the shirt, alternating between soft caresses and pinches, and watched them grow harder. When she moaned, it was my undoing. Whatever shred of control I'd been hanging onto was gone.

After raising my body so that I could remove her shirt, I said, "Your hands stay here until I tell you that you can move."

"I thought you had handcuffs."

My lip twitched. "You don't know what I have. Don't move, got it?"

"Yes." She quickly nodded her head, and I would have pointed out that she looked almost like a bobblehead doll when she'd done it, but I was way too gone to even form the words.

I kissed her again so the only sounds I could hear from her were moans caused by what I was inflicting on her body. I used my hand to place one of her nipples in my mouth. I sucked hard and bit down on the stiff peak enough to cause a gasp from Raven. Then, I slowly circled the tender area with my tongue until she began to moan. I was well aware of the thin line between pleasure and pain. She enjoyed it when I teased her like this.

My other hand coasted down her body until it met her pussy. My fingers danced along the pajama pants she had on, teasing her with what was to come.

My touch became more aggressive before I slipped my hand into her pants and was met with the cotton fabric of her underwear. After I changed positions to give her other nipple the same attention, I felt her heated gaze watch me as I continued to tease her, not dipping beyond the barrier that her panties provided. Before she could hide her eyes from me, I could see the yearning in them. I bet I could get her to beg for my touch if I wanted to. But that would require me having more patience than I did right now.

"What do you want?"

"I want you to—" She clamped her jaw shut tight before finishing the thought.

I was surprised that she said that much. "You want me to do what?"

I saw her mouth open once and then close. When she did it again, it was obvious that she was struggling to form the words.

"I—I want you—"

"I'm not doing anything else until I hear you say what we both want to hear."

"I want you to fuck me! First with your fingers and then with your cock!"

Her words fueled the fire burning within me. Who was I to deny her when she said it so sweetly?

I licked my lips and said, "Finally."

I leaned back and yanked her pajama pants and underwear down her legs. I was so hungry for her that I couldn't give her exactly what she wanted. At least not right away.

I ran a finger up and down her slit. "Fuck, you're soaked. You loved having me chase you, didn't you? Me claiming you as mine?"

"I'm not yours, Nash. I was once but not anymore."

"That's where you're wrong, Little Bird. And I'm willing to bet that was one of the reasons why you came back to Brentson. You were flying back home. To me."

Before she could think of a response, my mouth took my finger's place, and she groaned in delight. I would never tire of hearing that sound.

I enjoyed using my tongue to play with her clit.

"Please. Oh my—"

Her voice sounded desperate, and it forced me to look up at her from the task at hand. I was proud of her for having kept her hands where I had told her to, but I could see the growing struggle she was facing.

"You're free to move your hands," I said against her pussy. And then I went back to working her body into a frenzy.

She sighed in relief as her hands made their way into my hair. I groaned against her, and she shivered in response.

The cries that fell from her lips continued to build and I slid a finger into her. I slowly slipped another finger inside her with the first. I fought back the groan I wanted to release when I felt the walls of her pussy flutter against them. I could tell she was getting close.

I used my fingers to fuck her into oblivion and the look of pure bliss on her face was immaculate. If there were only a few images I could remember for the rest of my life, this would be one of them. I added another finger inside of her and she moaned.

"I'm going to—"

Those were the words I'd been waiting to hear. Her warning only served as encouragement, and when I felt her lose control of herself, my fingers and tongue didn't stop until she did.

While she caught her breath for a second, I dug into the bedside drawer and pulled out a condom. I quickly removed my clothes, not caring where they landed, and rolled the condom over my cock.

"I want you on your hands and knees facing the headboard."

The glazed look in her eyes made me wonder if she'd heard me but she complied. Once she was settled, I reached over and spanked her on the ass.

"Hey! What was that for?"

"Running. Although now we both know how much you like to be chased, Little Bird."

I slapped her on the ass three more times, and each time, her moans became louder. I took my cock and ran it up and down her slit, coating myself in her juices before burying myself deep inside of her.

"Yes!" she screamed after I'd finally given her what she wanted.

"This is going to be hard and fast and that is your only warning."

Before she could take another breath, my hands had tightened around her waist to help steady both of us before I started pounding into her. The pace I'd set went from zero to one hundred quickly and when she began to meet my thrusts, I groaned.

I could barely hear her cries over the sound of my pounding heart. This couldn't be described as anything but magical, and I was determined to enjoy every second of it.

Soon, her pussy clenched around my cock, I knew that she was almost there. That gave me another surge of energy and my thrusts became harder, determined to make sure that we were both going to come together.

As her orgasm took over her body, I pounded into her a couple more times before I joined her in an orgasmic induced haze. Mission complete.

Neither one of us moved for a minute as we tried to catch our breaths. She whined when I removed my cock from her body and walked away to throw out the evidence of our fucking. I wet a washcloth under warm water and walked back into the bedroom to help her get cleaned up before taking care of myself.

Once she was lying quietly in my arms, I couldn't help but say, "Looks like you're going to need another shower."

Her soft chuckles were the second sweetest sound I'd heard tonight.

9

RAVEN

I squinted at the light that was beaming down on my face. I was convinced that whoever allowed this to shine on me was doing it to piss me off. I'd slowly opened my eyes and found the culprit. The lamp on the nightstand closest to where I slept at night was on and it woke me from the short nap I'd taken. Although it wasn't long, it was the most peaceful slumber I'd had since I arrived at this cabin.

I wasn't surprised I had fallen asleep. I attributed it to the phenomenal sex Nash and I had tonight. Hate sex would do that to a person. I shook my head at myself when I thought about what Nash and I had done together tonight. Did we still hate each other? I could say that we did with a resounding yes. But he sure didn't treat my body like he hated it, or me, given the number of orgasms he'd given me. So why should I complain?

What the mind-blowing sex didn't cancel out was all the fucked-up things Nash had done. I'd been able to push that aside to fulfill my selfish needs a couple of hours ago, but that didn't make any of what he did okay.

Did I regret what happened tonight?

No.

As much as it pained me to say it, I would do it all over again in a heartbeat. The way our bodies melded to one another was hard to put into words. Even after spending two years apart, he knew my body in a way that shouldn't make sense but did.

But what I couldn't wrap my head around was him having no problem having sex with someone who he'd thought had betrayed him and tried to sleep with his father. To me, that would be the ultimate slap in the face, and I wouldn't want to see that person again, let alone blackmail them into a sexual relationship.

In his mind, was this a way for him to be able to compete with his father? Was it another source of revenge and payback?

Also, I still hadn't figured out what my feelings on all of this were yet. The things he made my body feel were out of this world, but guilt, for a multitude of reasons, still reigned supreme in my mind. Guilt from enjoying how he made me feel while we fucked. Guilt from the secrets I continued to keep because I was too afraid to speak about them.

Not to mention, I didn't trust Nash. He claimed to be concerned for my safety, forced me into staying in this cabin with him, yet I watched him slit a man's throat with a smile on his face just a few nights ago. How could I trust him after that?

What none of this answered was who would want to

kidnap me? And where did my mother's death fit into any of this, if it did at all?

I ran my hands across my face before I stretched my limbs, enjoying the feel of it throughout my body. Although I was slightly sore, I felt wonderful and relaxed. I tossed the covers off my body and got out of the bed. I found a white t-shirt that Nash had been wearing earlier that day and pulled it over my naked body. After I double checked that I hadn't missed him when I glanced at the bathroom, I walked out of the bedroom and found Nash sitting on the couch. The television was on, but I was pretty sure he wasn't actually watching what was on display. His head was down and the volume on the television was turned down low, so I assumed it was mostly just for background noise.

It would be easy for me to walk away and go back to bed, but something was pulling me toward him. Something I couldn't describe. It felt like there was a bond between us that seemed to never go away. Against every instinct of mine that was telling me to run in the opposite direction, I kept feeling as though something was pulling me back to him.

I walked into the living room and sat down on the couch, making sure to keep at least some space between us.

"Hey," I said. When Nash acknowledged my presence with a slight head nod, I continued, "Is everything all right?"

"Sure."

"Doesn't sound like it is, so that means it obviously isn't," I said matter-of-factly. It wasn't easy for me to hear that he was hiding something and for some reason, I wanted to know what.

"That's a valid assumption."

Why was he being cryptic? "Then, if you want to, tell me what's wrong."

"It's not something I want to talk about."

I should have expected him to not want to talk to me about what might be bothering him, but the rejection still hurt.

"Well, if it's all right, can I ask you a question?"

He nodded his head again. "Yes, but there's no guarantee that I'll answer it."

Fair.

"If you thought that I'd tried to sleep with your father, then why would you want to ever fuck me again?"

Nash didn't answer immediately, and I wondered if he was going to even answer at all. He leaned his head back and stretched his legs out in front of him before crossing them at the ankle.

He then turned his head toward me and said, "Part of it had to do with pride. I needed to show you that I was the one that could give you all the pleasure you'd ever need."

"Or it sounds like you needed to prove something to yourself."

That must have stung because his eyes narrowed at me. I'd known what I was doing when I said it and it came from the fact that I was angry that he would believe I'd stooped so low as to try to sleep with his father.

"I just can't wrap my head around you thinking I could do that to you, Nash."

"It wasn't so hard for me to believe. I never would have believed that you'd leave in the middle of the night without a word either, but here we are."

Nash's declaration forced me to do a double take. The way

he said it was so calculated. It had a coldness to it I wasn't expecting. He didn't owe me any loyalty, nor did he have any reason to trust in me after all of this time, but I'd be lying if I said his words didn't feel like a slap in the face.

Before all of this erupted, I'd been debating telling Nash the reason why I'd left, but something had been holding me back. I was glad that I listened to my instincts because I could only imagine what the ramifications would have been if I'd spilled everything, especially if he wasn't in the mental space to give me a fair shot at telling him my side of the story.

I held back what I really wanted to mention and instead said, "I never gave you the impression I would do such a thing. When we first got together in high school, I was nervous about what people might think about us being together. We grew up very differently and I didn't know what I was getting into with your father being the mayor of this town."

Fire blazed in his eyes. The ticking in his jaw became more prominent and I knew that none of this was going to end well. "I did everything I could to reassure you about how I felt about you. How I felt about us. But it wasn't good enough if you could even think of—"

"Don't even fucking say it. At this point it doesn't matter what I say, you're not going to believe me anyway so I'm not going to try."

I stood up to leave but he grabbed my hand before I could take a step.

"I want you to look me right in my eyes and tell me that you didn't try to fuck my dad."

With a deep sigh, I turned to face him, and it seemed perfectly fitting that I was the one looking down on him this time around. He'd made me feel like shit as soon as I'd stepped foot back into Brentson, and it was time to make him realize how it felt to be looked down on. It was probably a feeling that he'd never felt in his entire life.

"I didn't try, nor would I ever try, to sleep with your father. The very thought is revolting. And the fact that you still believe it, shows how little you think of me. In this case, the apple didn't fall too far from the tree, because you're disgusting just like your father."

I could feel him burning a hole into my back as I walked away from him. When I reached the bedroom again, I took some of the extra pillows that had been tossed on the floor and created a wall between my side of the bed and what would be his. I didn't know if he would come in here after what had happened in the living room, but I wanted to be fully prepared just in case. If he didn't get the hint that he wasn't welcome here after my last comment, then this should do the trick.

But what he didn't know was that guilt had crawled into my subconscious.

Because, while what I'd said was true, I still hadn't told him everything.

10

NASH

I replayed the conversation that I'd had with Raven in my head over and over again, long after she'd retreated into the cabin's only bedroom. I'd been in a shitty mood after our interaction and deep down I knew I shouldn't have taken it out on her. She was simply the closest target and I'd done everything I could to make sure she felt the same way I did.

Why had I done it?

I'd shut her out. Part of it was because I was still pissed at her for trying to escape. There had been no doubt in my mind that she was going to try to leave, which was why I'd threatened her before. I knew my words only helped fertilize the seed that had been planted in her head. What I hadn't expected was for her to attempt to murder me with a glass while she tried to make her "grand escape."

But there was something else. What I didn't want her to know was that I'd felt vulnerable. I didn't want to let her in. The last time I had, she'd disappeared without a trace, and I was left dealing with the fallout. People constantly asking how I was doing ended up being a burden instead of a comfort. The intrusive questions about her disappearance went on for months, making it impossible to let it go and move on. Trying to come up with answers to those questions while everyone looked at me with pity left me constantly pissed off.

The memories of those months irritated me and that mixed with the new anger I felt toward Raven over the current situation was enough to make me do something emotional. I left my place on the couch and walked into the kitchen to grab a beer. That would give me something to do.

I retrieved the beer out of the fridge and used a beer opener to pop the top off. The freshness from the cold brew coated my throat and slightly lessened my anger. I took the bottle and strolled out of the kitchen and the front door.

Was it silly to go outside with the weather as cool as it was? Yes, but if it meant that it would cool me down, then so be it. The sounds of nature that surrounded me as soon as I stepped outdoors might be a concern for some, but it was peaceful to me.

Being alone out here had become my safe haven when things became stressful, but with Raven in the house, it felt as if my world had been turned upside down. I was still fighting with myself about whether or not she tried to sleep with my father. When my father found me heartbroken after I'd discovered that Raven was gone and he'd told me why she left, I'd had no doubts in my mind about that being the case. I hadn't considered anything else.

I hated that the thought of her and my father was still there, floating around my brain whenever things in my head grew quiet. It had become more apparent since she'd arrived back in town, which made sense. I'd tried to forget about it, but with her back here, it dug up every memory and thought I had about her that I was hoping had been buried.

It was a huge problem. Ever since she'd been back in town, she'd done nothing but fuck with my head, and this was a time in my life that should have been dedicated to school, football, and the Chevaliers. I'd hoped and wished for her to come back years ago and now that she was here, she'd caused nothing but stress. Having her here made me want to fall back into the old habits that we used to have, but I was still pissed. My feelings about her lulled between what we used to have and being angry about the current state of things.

I took another gulp of beer as I scanned my surroundings. I could imagine that my grandfather did the same thing when his emotions got the best of him. I could see him wandering on this porch, lost in thought, as he tried to come up with an answer that eluded him.

I finished my beer off before I stepped back inside, hoping that an answer would come to me sooner rather than later. The irritation and anger were still there but taking the same steps that my grandfather had walked numerous times and being outside had made me feel lighter. For the time being.

I walked into the bedroom and found her sleeping peacefully on her side. She was curled up into a ball. I couldn't help but wonder if it was a comfort thing or if she was trying to make herself smaller after what I'd said.

Get a fucking grip, Henson. That position is just comfortable for her.

Raven had put a bunch of pillows behind her, creating a

makeshift barrier between us. I knew she was doing it to be more symbolic of the gulf between the two of us, because that wouldn't remotely keep me from grabbing her if I wanted to. Having to be separated from her for this length of time now felt suffocating. The urge to be near her was as constant as my need to breathe. I knew that was fucking with my brain as well.

That was when an idea popped into my head. It was sooner than I expected it to happen, and I was glad. Raven needed to learn that I meant what I said and said what I meant. I'd respect her desire to put space between us, but we would do it my way.

As if she knew I was watching her, she turned her body and flipped onto her back, *Perfect.* It was as if the stars were aligning and knew what my plan was.

I left the bedroom and went back to the black duffel I'd asked Easton to bring. I'd had him grab a black case that was meant to be a surprise for Raven, but I had no problem "surprising" her now. She wouldn't be happy about it, but I didn't care.

I unzipped the small case and took out what I needed. I walked back into the bedroom and was pleased to see that she hadn't moved again. This would make my job a hell of a lot easier.

I didn't think about what I was doing as I moved. If I stalled for any moment of time, it could lead to her waking up before I had a chance to enact my plan. The deepness of her breathing told me that she was soundly asleep as I grabbed her wrist and handcuffed it to the bed. I thanked my lucky stars that we hadn't bothered replacing the bed frame after my grandfather died because if we had, this solution wouldn't be possible.

I pulled the covers back and got into the bed. I reached my hand back and touched the pillows. Instinct made me want to pull her into my arms, but I refrained. Instead I chose to fall into a restless sleep.

11

RAVEN

I knew something was wrong even before I woke up. It was as if my body sensed that something was amiss, but I couldn't tell what it was.

Or at least I couldn't until I moved my left hand.

I tried to pull my arm to me, but it was being held back by something. That was when I opened my eyes and saw that I was handcuffed to the bed.

That son of a b—

"Nash!" I yelled at the top of my lungs. "Hey, asshole, let me go!"

When he didn't immediately appear or respond, my brain immediately went into panic mode. Was he even in the cabin? Had he left me here chained to a fucking bed? I went back to yelling.

"Help! Help!"

It was then that I heard the bedroom door open and in strolled Nash with a mug in his hand.

"Good morning," he said with a smirk on his face.

Anger built in my body as I took in his stance before me.

Him appearing to be cool, calm, and relaxed while I was in this predicament only added more fuel to the flames that were building in my body. "How dare you do this to me? Uncuff me."

"Nah, I don't feel like it." He took a sip of whatever was in the cup. It was as if he had all the time in the world and that me being handcuffed to the bed was a normal, everyday occurrence.

"Why are you doing this?"

"It was meant to teach you a lesson."

"A lesson? Because I tried to escape?"

"Bingo."

"You are a sadistic bastard." Those were the first words I could think of and they flew out of my mouth with all the disgust I was feeling toward him.

"Wouldn't be the worst thing I've been called."

"Let. Me. Go." I yanked my arm, hoping that either the handcuffs or the bed frame would give way, allowing me to free myself. My hopes went unanswered. Instead, I felt the sharp sting of the cuffs digging into my wrist.

"I'll let you go... eventually. Once I calm down, that is."

"Once you calm down? You seem pretty fucking calm already."

"Then I guess we'll wait for you to chill the fuck out first."

I growled at him before asking, "And if I have to use the bathroom?"

"Sounds like a personal problem to me."

"It will become your problem when you have to clean it up."

"I won't be cleaning a damn thing."

Oh, that's right. It's because he was rich. The fact that he would have someone else clean my bodily waste that he could have easily let me loose to take care of was despicable and made me judge him even more harshly.

"Who's pulling a stunt now?"

When his gaze narrowed on me, I knew he hadn't been expecting that comeback. *Good.* It served him right for doing this. Instead of responding, he took another sip from his mug before turning to leave the room.

As I was about to yell at him again, he stopped, and looked over his shoulder and said, "Don't forget. This was only the first part of my threat. You aren't remotely prepared for the second half."

With that he left the room, closing the door behind him. I screamed in frustration and anger, but that too went unanswered.

I was bored out of my mind. I didn't have my phone since Nash hadn't returned it after kidnapping me and dragging me here, so I couldn't use that to distract me. After Nash walked out of the bedroom earlier and left me handcuffed in here like a criminal, I yelled at him to release me for what seemed like hours, but he just ignored me. After I accepted that he wasn't coming back until he was damn good and ready, I stopped screaming and settled in to wait for him. It didn't make sense for me to continue to lose my voice too, I already felt like I'd lost my dignity.

If he didn't get back in here soon, we were going to have another problem. My bladder was currently so full, I was sure I could hear it screaming at me inside my body. Although I wasn't excited at the prospect of peeing the bed I was currently cuffed to, it would serve that asshole right to have to deal with the mess. The idea of that almost made me smile, until I remembered he'd just call someone else to do it anyway.

As if he knew I was thinking about him, Nash waltzed into the room nonchalantly, as if he didn't have a care in the world and strolled over to my side of the bed. He sat down on the edge, and I maneuvered my body to try to kick him off.

"Calm down. I'm about to uncuff you." He held up a small key for me to see.

I froze in place and waited for him to follow through on his words. He took his sweet time moving toward the handcuffs, but he finally unlocked them with the key he was holding. When I heard the decisive click announcing I'd been freed, I quickly pulled my wrist out of the cuff and bolted out of the bed to go use the bathroom, slamming the door behind me. I'd made it just in time.

Once I'd finished emptying my bladder and washing up, I walked out and found Nash leaning against the doorframe connecting the living area and the bedroom.

"Have you learned your lesson?"

My stomach chose then to growl, and I knew I needed to eat as soon as possible. I wasn't sure how long I'd been cuffed to the bed while I was awake, but it had been hours since I'd woken up this morning. I was stiff and sore, I'd barely made it to the toilet on time, I was hungry and thirsty, and now he was going to stand here, talking to me like I was some petulant child who he'd sent to a time out? Well fuck that and fuck him. He had no right, and I was so far beyond mad I could barely see straight.

"Fuck your lessons. Now get out of my way."

Nash didn't even attempt to move away from the door.

"Nash, move." I could have been more polite, but I honestly didn't care anymore. I was beyond pissed and if he didn't move, I was bound to do something out of anger.

Nash just stood there, looking as if he couldn't care less about anything I said and I was over it. I walked up to the doorway where he was standing and pushed him out of the way. It would have probably been easier for me to answer his question, but I didn't care. I needed to do something to vent the rage I was feeling. I shoved him out of the doorway with all my might and it barely moved him a few inches, but it was still somewhat satisfying.

I was now free to go into the living area and I wasted no time making my way into the kitchen to find something to eat. I didn't hear Nash follow me into the kitchen, although I could feel his presence before I stood up straight and closed the refrigerator door. I'd found ingredients for a yogurt parfait that would at least take the edge off of my hunger. I tossed the ingredients together in a bowl and looked up. He was still standing there.

"Can I help you with something or are you going to just stand there and watch as I stuff my face?"

When he didn't reply, I rolled my eyes and walked over to the dining room table. I wasn't shocked to see him follow suit and pull out his own chair to sit down.

This was downright creepy. I knew this was his way of trying to intimidate me, but I refused to let him. I did, however, slightly change my approach. "Is there something I can help you with?"

He raised his eyebrows slightly before he leaned back in

the chair and folded his arms across his chest. A smirk found its way to his lips.

All he was doing was getting me further riled up. I hated that he had this power over me, but I told myself it was understandable after he'd just gotten done handcuffing me to a bed.

"So what's on your agenda? Kidnapping someone else?"

"Would that please you if I did?"

I snorted. "It would please me if you let me go."

"I already told you that's not happening. Not until I know you're—"

I slammed my fist down on the table. I swear I didn't have anger issues before coming back to Brentson. Or hell, since finding myself around Nash again.

"Safe." I put imaginary quotes around the word using my fingers. "I know. Safe from this threat that we aren't sure even still exists. I'm honestly convinced that you kidnapped me in some bullshit ploy to make me fall in love with you again."

I took another bite of my parfait. Eating was the only thing keeping me from completely losing my sanity.

"I wouldn't have to try hard at all for that, Little Bird."

A sarcastic chuckle left my mouth before I realized it happened. "You couldn't even get me to fuck you now if you tried to blackmail me into doing it again."

"Now we both know that that's a lie, Goodwin."

I almost lost all of my nerve when he said my name. His use of my last name meant that he was growing more irritated, but I couldn't back down. I refused to back down.

"After all, isn't this just a pissing contest that you have going on with your father about whether he'd fucked my brains out too?"

The words slipped out before I realized I was going to say them. The impact of what I said hit us both at the same time, but he reacted first. He hopped out of his chair, and it fell back with a resounding thud. My heart lurched into my throat, preventing me from screaming as he came toward me.

12

RAVEN

Nash snatched the spoon out of my hand before he grabbed me by the forearms and pulled me until I was standing. We were standing so close together that I thought he was going to kiss me, but he didn't. He bent down and tossed me over his shoulder.

"What in the world—"

"You wanted to piss me off? Well, congrats, you've done it. Now it's time for you to face the consequences."

I balled my hand into a fist and started beating on his back. I could feel the anger radiating off of him and I thrived on it. Getting him as pissed as he'd made me was fucking thrilling. He'd tried to assert his dominance throughout our entire stay here and I'd had enough. Every step he took sounded thunderous as he carried me back into the bedroom. When he tossed me on the bed, I immediately scrambled to get up from the mattress, but Nash used his body to stop me.

"Stop fucking moving."

"Hell no. Get off of me."

"You didn't listen to my warning."

I swallowed hard. I thought about what the rest of his threat was, and it sent a shiver through my body.

Nash's gaze on me darkened before he said, "You wanted my attention. You got it."

I hated my body's reaction to him. I hated that I wanted to fight him and fuck him at the same damn time.

"You can try to fight it, but you don't want to leave this bed and you can't wait to see what I'm about to do to you."

"And all you want to do is fuck me to shut me up."

The grin that appeared on Nash's face was anything but friendly. "I'm glad we're on the same page. I want you on your knees, ass facing me."

Try that stunt again, and I'll have no problem handcuffing you to that bed in there and spanking that ass of yours until you can barely walk.

Fuck. He'd spanked me after I tried to get away in the SUV, but it wasn't near enough to make it so I couldn't walk. Now it seemed as if he was going to carry through with his promise.

I felt him roughly pull down my pants and flip me to my knees in one swift motion. I should have been more pissed about what was about to happen, but I was excited. I could feel myself growing wetter and he'd barely touched me. Feeling my body's betrayal caused a huge contradiction within me. He'd turned me against myself and was ready to use it to his advantage.

His hand softly caressed my butt. "I'm going to spank you until this ass turns pink. And then I'm going to fuck you so hard that you won't know which way is up or down."

If I thought I was wet before, I was soaked now. Nash's

finger moved from touching my ass to running a finger up and down my seam. "You liked that, didn't you? I can feel that you're soaked through your panties."

Before I could react, his hand slapped my ass, and it seemed as if I could hear the sound echoing all around the room. I gasped in response, and I could hear Nash chuckling behind me. It made me want to throttle him, but my traitorous body was too invested in whatever this was to distract either of us by going after him.

"That slap was for not paying attention to my warning. I'm doing this for your damn safety even if you're too hardheaded to listen." He shifted my panties down so that my butt cheeks were exposed.

"Telling someone they are hardheaded is—"

He slapped my ass again and I squealed. It had been harder than the first time and that was unexpected. But he was nowhere near done. He used the palm of his hand to briefly caress the stinging area before smacking the opposite cheek sharply.

After that, a couple more slaps came quickly, followed by Nash's hands rubbing my ass cheeks gently again. He repeated the spanking and caressing a few more times, and I was grateful he hadn't asked me to count them because there was no way I would have been able to keep track. The way he kept me riding a knife's edge between pain and pleasure was making it impossible to think, I could only feel.

I tried to hold back sounds or words but failed. I loved what Nash was doing to me as much as I hated him for doing it. Tears appeared in the corner of my eyes, but I wasn't hurt. I was losing the battle to control myself and the fight was becoming too much. When the tears drifted down my face, I felt him move my panties out the way before he touched my pussy.

"You're fucking soaked. I love it."

Hearing his satisfaction over my body's response to what he'd done made my stomach turn into one big knot. I could hope and wish that what he said wasn't true, but I knew it was. His fingers played along my seam before he stuck them into me. I heard him mumble a curse under his breath. And then he moved his hand, and I was all but gone.

"Nash," his name fell off my lips and ended with a groan. Soon it became part of a chant that drifted between saying his name and making an indescribable noise that I probably couldn't repeat unless I was in this state.

"This is all you're going to think about when you sit down. How sore I've made your ass and how much you enjoyed it."

"Yes," I said, but lost my train of thought. If there was even a train of thought because of what he was doing to me. The only thing I could think about was where he was touching me and the sensations he was sending through my body. The pleasure in me began to build from the combination of the spanking and him fucking me with his fingers. It wouldn't take long for me to reach my climax and it was the only thing I was hanging onto. I needed this. I craved this.

I closed my eyes as a groan left my lips and I could feel my body ready to accept the orgasm that was about to rip through it. Nash must have sensed it too because then he stopped his movements. My eyes popped back open, and I looked over my shoulder. I saw him smirking as he studied me.

"You thought I was going to let you come that easy? You have to earn it."

Nash chose that moment to slap my pussy, sending a jolt through my entire body. What the hell was he doing to me?

"Fuck you," were the only words I could get out.

I heard Nash chuckle behind me. "No, Little Bird. I will be fucking you. Finish taking off your pants and panties."

I did as he said, and he tossed something near my body on the bed. It only took a second for me to put together what it was. "You bought me a vibrator?"

"And you're going to use it on your clit while I fuck you. Get back into position."

I should have been turned off because of the way he'd spoken to me. But I wasn't. In fact, I couldn't tell you if I was more turned on now or more turned on when he was spanking my ass. I heard him rip open what I assumed was a condom wrapper behind me.

I found the vibrator and the remote and got back on my knees. Nash moved my legs further apart before he joined me on the bed.

"Do as I said, Raven. Put the toy on your clit and don't move it until I say so."

I stared the toy down before I put it near my clit. I used my other hand to press the button to start the device. When the toy turned on, I moved my hand because I was surprised by the vibration, and I could hear Nash growling behind me before I put the object back where he wanted it.

He ran his cock up and down my seam and I waited in anticipation for him to slide into me. When he did, I cried out.

"Oh, my—"

My words dropped off because my ability to speak died. He moved his body back slightly before he slammed into me.

I was stunned into complete silence. I felt completely full and him fucking me was just beginning. When he pounded into me again, I screamed.

"I'm coming."

"Good. Because that won't be the first time that happens today."

If all of the foreplay before this had been adding kindling to the fire, his words lit the match. I soon felt myself sliding over the edge to the point of no return and I enjoyed every second of it.

"Keep the vibrator where it is."

I did as he asked, and it took me a moment to catch my breath again. When I did, I said, "Please..."

"Please what?" he said as he pounded into me again.

"I want to come again."

Nash growled in return and picked up his pace. I didn't want this to end as my eyes drifted closed because I could feel the pleasure building up within me once more. I couldn't have another orgasm this quickly, could I?

"Nash." My voice trailed off because once again, words eluded me.

"I know. I'm right there with you."

It took no time before I felt my entire body tighten and then relax once more as my orgasm took over. When Nash let out a groan, I knew that he had followed me off the edge and was sailing into a world of relaxation and bliss.

Nash didn't move right away. He took his time catching his breath before he slipped out of me, and I immediately missed the feel of him inside of me. I collapsed on the bed, and I could hear him moving around in the bathroom, but I had no energy to try to see what he was doing.

I didn't bother trying to watch him come back into the room, but I heard him. I also felt when he took a warm washcloth and cleaned me, making sure to use the washcloth to soothe my ass. I jumped when I felt his hands massage my butt cheeks and there was something on them.

"This is just lotion. To help with the sting."

I was too tired to argue, and it felt wonderful. As he continued to pay close attention to my ass, I couldn't help but reflect on what had just happened. The first hate-fuck session, I didn't have any concerns about it at all. But this one? I knew it would take no time before I ended up regretting it. Specifically, regretting how much I enjoyed it.

13

NASH

The yawn that left my mouth couldn't be avoided. Although I'd gotten a decent amount of sleep the night before, I'd woken up early and still felt exhausted. It didn't help that I was pissed at myself. I was supposed to be focused on studying for an exam, yet I found myself constantly glancing at Raven, in hopes of getting her attention. But she continued to not give me the time of day.

It had been like this ever since I'd fucked the hell out of her after she pressed my buttons once I'd uncuffed her from the bed. To make matters even more interesting, we'd never settled the big argument we had the other night about what really happened between her and my father. I knew we had a lot to discuss, and knowing Raven and her likely state of mind, it wasn't going to be a pleasant conversation. At first, I was okay with the silence. I didn't blame her for ignoring me, but it was driving me bat shit crazy.

As the silence continued on, I started to question my father's version of what happened. I didn't fully understand why I was having a change of heart, but I was starting to believe Raven. What had caused this change?

I wasn't exactly sure, but the dig she'd thrown at me, where she mentioned the pissing contest with my father, had hit harder than I thought either one of us expected it would. To have the audacity to throw that in there after she'd denied that it had occurred has caused a shift in me. It was as if she'd had nothing to lose and didn't care about the consequences... well at least she didn't until I spanked her ass until it was pink.

I could admit that I shouldn't have treated her the way I had, but after believing what my father had said for so long, it had been hard to rewire my brain to think otherwise. I'd tried to talk to her when she stepped out into the living room this morning and I got no response. I went as far as trying to piss her off by teasing her that I would give her back her phone if she spoke to me, but she refused to give in. And I was too far above begging to get her to talk to me that way.

At least for now I was.

I attributed my feelings to being in such small confinements with her over the last few days. The only person I could talk to face-to-face right now was her and she was ignoring me. Normally, being alone and not having to deal with anyone would be a nice feeling for me but for some reason, it was bugging me when it came to her. I could lie to myself and say it's because of our shared history and our involvement in a stressful situation.

But I knew what the real reason was. It was just because it was her. Not being able to speak to her while she was away had been horrible and I couldn't help but wonder what she was doing at that exact moment. Now I knew what she was doing. Attempting to focus on reading the textbook in front of her even though she'd been on the same page for the last twenty minutes.

And that was frustrating as hell.

The other thing that angered me? I still hadn't figured out who sent Paul after her. You would think that my killing of him would have had someone step out and try to come after Raven again and, by extension, me. As far as we knew, no one had. It made the whole situation more peculiar.

I'd asked Tomas to see if he might have been able to find out more information, given that he had a much wider net of connections due to his position, but he hadn't gotten back to me. Until I heard more, we were staying put. Which meant I had to deal with the shit that Raven was throwing at me. For now.

Having her barrel back into my life had shown me how empty my life had been without her in it. In her absence, those moments where I'd had big celebrations or shitty days made me feel almost numb because she wasn't there to partake, or I hadn't been able to tell her what happened. Suddenly it hit me, almost like the glass hit the wall the other day when she threw it at me: I still loved her.

Even with all the bullshit, I still loved her.

I was jerked out of my thoughts when I saw movement out of the corner of my eye, and I knew this was my chance. She placed her textbook on the coffee table in front of her, so I gently pushed my seat back so that I was ready to move when she did.

When she stood up and left the room, I snatched a small bottle out of the black duffel bag on the floor next to me and followed her. My stride ate up the distance between us and I cornered her near the wall just outside the bedroom.

"What the hell do you want?"

My lip twitched. "Ah, so she does speak."

"I have no problem speaking. I just didn't *want* to speak to you. And you obviously can't take a hint."

"That was obvious and now I'm going to make sure you do."

"So, once again, when you don't get your way, you have to force someone to do something they don't want to do."

Her comment did sting a little, but she wasn't wrong. I handed her the small bottle in my hand, and she looked at it and then me with wide eyes.

"You remembered to get my medicine?"

"Of course I did. I assumed you might be taking medicine for your ADHD, so I asked Easton to grab it when he was at your house. After I saw you reading the same page over and over again and pulling at your hair, it reminded me that I'd asked him to do so."

She didn't say anything as she took the bottle out of my hand and just stared at it. That only increased my frustration.

"For someone who almost got kidnapped and potentially killed, you sure are being ungrateful for what I've done for you."

She did a double take. "I should be grateful? You did the exact same thing! You could have easily taken me back to my house on campus, but instead you want to keep me here for who knows how long."

"I already told you, we don't know who sent Paul after you. So it's best that we keep a low profile until we do."

"How do I know this isn't some elaborate scheme that you

put together?"

My eyes narrowed. "Do you think I would go through all of this trouble?"

"I don't know. You tell me. You seemed awfully happy to kill him."

"I had nothing to do with the attempt to kidnap you and I've been trying to get to the bottom of it since we got here."

"Why do you care anyway? You don't give a shit about me. So you could easily just let me go. I'm willing to pretend like this never happened. I'm way past ready to get back to my real life, whatever that looks like now anyway." I could sense the sadness in her voice.

"Give me a day or two more to see if I can find anything, and if not, I'll bring you back to Brentson."

I could see the distrust in her eyes, and I didn't blame her. I wouldn't trust me either if I were her.

"I'm holding you to it. We go back to Brentson after I've 'miraculously recovered' and we can tell everyone that we broke up again so that no one wonders why we aren't seen with each other in the future."

"That makes perfect sense. You have yourself a deal, Goodwin."

I held out my hand for her to shake as if this was an agreement between the two of us. What she didn't know was that there was a card that I held in my back pocket. The one where I was going to convince her that this fake dating bullshit no longer existed.

No, this was the real deal. More than just hot, passionate sex. I needed for her to see that the dreams we talked about in high school could still be our reality. With everything in me, I was determined to show her that she was mine.

14

RAVEN

I was still thinking about Nash making sure that I had my ADHD medication while we were stuck here as I brushed my hair in the bathroom mirror, braiding my wet strands into a single braid down my back. I'd just gotten out of the shower that I randomly decided to take. The hope had been to calm the thoughts racing through my mind, but I'd failed.

Him being considerate about my medication wasn't enough to make me forget about the fact that he'd murdered someone and kidnapped me. Not to mention him being a complete asshole the evening before. I'd tried to distract myself from the conflicting feelings I had but was left worn down and confused.

I wished that I'd had more time with my mom every day, but specifically during moments like this. Moments when her wisdom would have been something I would have almost traded anything for. She would have just the right thing to say even if she didn't know the answer or what the outcome would be.

Hell, if she were still here, I wouldn't be in this predicament to begin with. I would have made wiser choices, I would have stayed in Brentson, and I wouldn't have been forced to come back here in order to find out the truth about what happened to my mother.

Part of me wondered if this was all a ruse. That there wasn't an underlying mystery surrounding my mother's death.

No.

I couldn't give up hope. Someone went through a lot of hoops to get me back here and I needed to remain positive that I would have my questions answered.

Once I was done with the braid, I was going to make a second attempt at doing some of my homework in the bedroom. I didn't want to take my medication for fear that it would keep me up the rest of the night, but now having the option to do so made me feel a mix of emotions. Well, a bigger mix of emotions because I already felt as if I was walking on a tightrope, and who knew where I would land if I fell off.

Nash was still in the living room area, doing who knows what, but I needed a break from him. Since the only way I was going to get done was to not be in the same room as him, this was about as good as it was going to get.

I thought that some space apart would have allowed me the ability to see things more clearly, but I was still in a muddled headspace. I wish I could snap my fingers and have the answer to everything that was going on in my life, but it would never be that simple.

I exited the bathroom and walked over to my side of the bed. As I was about to pick up my laptop and get comfortable, I saw that something had fallen behind the bed. It took some maneuvering on my end to get it.

When I yanked it from its resting place, I was met with a lot of dust. I tried to keep my mouth closed as I fought to control my sneeze. I couldn't help but wonder how long it had been back there.

After wiping some of the dust off, I read the cover of the book and gasped. It was a small, thin journal that had Chevaliers written across the top. I glanced at the door, knowing that at any moment, Nash could walk in and spot me with the journal. Deep down, I knew this was an opportunity I couldn't let go to waste. Who knew what lay between these pages and I couldn't wait to find out.

I looked at the bedroom door again to see if it had some sort of lock on it. It would be odd for me to lock the door, but it would stop him long enough for me to hide the book. When I didn't see anything, I got up and walked over there just to be sure, but there was no way to lock the door.

Oh shit. Nash really could walk in at any moment, and I wouldn't have much time to prepare to hide it. I was determined to read it, so it was a risk I was willing to take. I got back on the bed and turned onto my side with my back facing the door so if I heard the doorknob turn, I would at least be able to block him from seeing what I was doing while I hopefully had an opportunity to slide the book underneath my pillow. I opened the book to the first page and started reading. I almost immediately got lost in exploring some of the Chevaliers' history.

The book made sure to note that this wasn't an all-inclusive history of the Chevaliers. It did mention that it was founded by three men that I'd never heard of. They'd wanted to promote brotherhood between its members and laid the foundation to form those bonds within the organization. It didn't explain no one batting an eye at Nash murdering a man in their home though. Not that I expected it to.

I was fascinated by the words I was reading. The fact that this wasn't in Brentson's library was a shame, but maybe that was for good reason. Then again, at least some of the members of the organization had no problem with committing crimes such as blackmail and murder. The book didn't mention this, but given how comfortable Nash was with killing someone, I began to wonder if murder was a requirement for entry.

I'd soon discovered that I wasn't wrong. After reading further into the book, the author talked about bloodshed that had come about as a result of battles that Chevaliers had in order to protect their interests. It seemed as if most of their interests surrounded more ways to gain money, whether by legal or illegal means.

I closed my eyes and cringed after reading a scene that was particularly gruesome, involving torturing someone by cutting out their eyeballs for being a spy and telling trade secrets to an opponent of the Chevaliers. Why would anyone write this down in a book? They were basically admitting to crimes and clearly didn't give a damn. If this ended up in the wrong hands, then some people might be arrested for the crimes they committed.

I realized the Chevaliers didn't have to worry about things like arrests and convictions though. The people who were mentioned in this book moved in circles that were essentially above the law, and they didn't give a damn who knew what they'd done. They didn't have to think about consequences.

People like this just knew there were no consequences for them. That was perhaps the most frightening part because that meant they had nothing to lose.

The torture brought me back to what Nash had done to my would-be kidnapper, and I thought about how dark that evening could have turned out if Nash hadn't decided to end it when he did. The people in this organization had no issue with doing what they seemed fit. That actually made me fear for whoever else might be involved in the plot to kidnap me.

The book shared information on prominent members within the society, including the Cross family, who I vaguely knew about because of how rich they were and their ties to Brentson University. It was not surprising that they were a part of the Chevaliers, given that they seemed to have a shit ton of money and they ran in the same circles as the Hensons.

I still didn't understand why this book had been left here where anyone could find it? Even if the Chevaliers weren't afraid of paying for their crimes, keeping a record like this, and leaving it lying around seemed reckless. Then again, I assumed that Nash's grandfather hadn't expected someone outside of their family to be staying in this cabin.

When I turned the page again, I found an older photo of Nash, Bianca, and who I assumed was their grandfather. They were sitting on what looked like the front porch of the cabin and had their arms around each other with huge smiles on their faces. I knew that this was before we were dating because his grandfather had already passed away when we had started dating and Nash looked to barely be in his teens, if that.

If his grandfather cared about the Chevaliers as much as I

suspected he did, just based on what little I knew about Nash's involvement, he probably held them in high regard and enough for him to put a treasured photo of his grandkids in a book to protect it. I stuffed the photo back into where it was and turned the page.

What was in this book felt like only the tip of the iceberg for this organization and the words that were on the page kept me so engaged that I didn't want to stop. As I went to turn the page, I heard a loud thump outside my bedroom door. I jumped and stuffed the book under my pillow. This was what I feared would happen.

Before I could regulate my heartbeat after the jump scare, the door flew open, and Nash walked in. I was confused about why he'd walked in here since he usually left me to my own devices in the bedroom until he decided to come to bed. This time, however, he'd come into the bedroom with something in his hands. The moment I saw what it was, my mouth dropped open and I hopped out of bed, forgetting all about what I'd been doing only a moment before.

"Where'd you get this from?" I asked as I walked over to him. I was nervous about asking, given what I'd just been reading and how he usually shut me down when I asked him a question anyway.

"Delivery, I couldn't get us cones because it needed to be easy to transport. Don't get me started on how difficult it was to actually get someone to deliver it to the main cabin and then to have one of the staff drive it down here." He handed me a cup of ice cream from Smith's Ice Cream Parlor, and I noticed it was my favorite flavor, birthday cake.

To say I was surprised was an understatement. Ever since our talk about how he didn't trust me, we've been walking on eggshells around each other, and I'd mostly been ignoring him. This was the first time since I'd been back that I felt completely at ease around him.

"Thank you. This is so thoughtful of you." I could, at least attempt to be nice.

"It's the least I could do," he said.

"What do you mean? The least that you could do?" I asked.

"Look, why don't we go and get some spoons and then eat this out in the living room. Then I can tell you what I want to say."

Who was this man standing before me? The hardened guy that I was coming to know seemed to, in some ways, be reverting to the boyfriend I used to have. "Sure. I'll be out in a second."

This change in behavior from Nash was enough to make me suspicious but I wasn't about to turn down an opportunity to have ice cream from Smith's Ice Cream Parlor. I hesitated for a second before walking out of the bedroom and joining Nash on the couch just as he placed two spoons on the coffee table in front of us. I grabbed a spoon before Nash could give it to me. Then I took the top off the ice cream cup and immediately dug in. The moan that left my lips was involuntary.

"I love that sound," Nash mumbled under his breath. I didn't know what to say in response, so I quietly kept eating the delicious treat in my hand.

"We had so many dates at Smith's."

Nash's words forced my head to turn toward him. This conversation had started off friendly and had taken me off guard. It was nice having a truce of sorts, but I couldn't help but wonder what he was really up to.

I nodded and said, "Yeah, we did. That was when life was simpler. Much simpler than it is now. And we had no idea how easy we had it."

It was before my life turned upside down and I had to flee. Before I had to say goodbye to the only place I'd ever called home and to the only man that had ever loved me.

"There's something else I want to give you."

He pulled out my phone from his pocket. "If you promise not to call anyone until we get the all-clear and sit with me until we finish this ice cream, I'll give it to you."

"Nash, I'm not a child and—"

"I know you're not. Just promise me this."

"Fine."

He handed it over without another word. After looking through my emails and text messages, I noticed that I had a ton of people I needed to get back to.

I put my phone in my lap and continued to eat my ice cream, wondering what the next catch would be. I was still suspicious of his change in behavior.

"Is it as good as you remember?"

"Yes. While I knew I missed it, I didn't realize how much I missed it until now."

"A lot of things changed after you left."

I turned to look at him and found him staring back at me. "I know, Nash. I know."

15

RAVEN

"You sound pretty good."

"Thank you?" I said as I put the phone down on the bathroom counter. After texting Izzy back and forth last night to confirm that I was okay, I decided to call her the next evening to chat while I took my hair out of its braid.

"I mean for someone that has been sick."

"I guess that's true. I'm feeling pretty much back to normal." I'd almost fucked up. I wanted to tell her the truth, but I didn't know what kind of danger I was putting her in if I did tell her what had actually happened to me. Then again, Nash had no problem telling Bianca and Easton what had happened so what was stopping me? Was this something you told someone over the phone?

"And I'm glad you were able to have Nash there to help. What was that like? I'd expected that he would be the last person who would want to help you."

Tell me something I don't know, please.

"Yeah, I can't complain, though. He knew I was in bad

shape when he found me, and once I was stable, he whisked me away to help me."

"Did you play find the stethoscope?"

I did a double take and stared at my phone. "Excuse me? Did you just refer to sex as that?"

"Maybe."

"We need to talk about your euphemisms."

"Regardless of that, don't try to change the subject!"

"Why would I be having sex when I was sick? That's exerting a lot of energy. And weren't you ready to beat up Nash when we were at that frat party?"

"That was before he decided to drop everything to take care of you. He clearly still cares about you. And you're clearly feeling better now and you're single, he's single, and it's not like you haven't fucked before so..."

I ran a hand over my face, immensely regretting when I told Izzy that I'd lost my virginity to Nash and that he'd come over to give me a "proper goodbye" without knowing that was what he was doing. Although she didn't know the real reason I was here, her sentiment was still true. He had done everything to be here with me, including murdering someone. Setting aside the fact that he looked like he actually enjoyed it, he didn't have to kill my would-be kidnapper on my behalf.

I cleared my throat and said, "That's not what is going on over here."

"Well maybe it should. It doesn't hurt to get laid every once in a while."

I rolled my eyes. "I'm going to hang up, Izzy. I'll see you soon."

"Stay as long as you want if it means you're—"

I hung up the phone, cutting her off mid-sentence.

I ran my fingers through my hair, loving the waves that had been created as a result of taking my braid out. After one final look in the mirror, I grabbed my phone and turned off the lights.

With the conversation that I'd had with Izzy at the front of my mind, I walked through the bedroom and into the living room and found Nash in his usual spot in the cabin: sitting on the couch. This time, however, he was on his laptop.

"Want to watch a movie on TV?" The question left my lips before I could stop it.

It seemed as if my question had shocked Nash as well because he slowly looked up from his laptop and turned to look at me. He gave me a once over and I felt my cheeks warm. His gaze stayed on the skin that was exposed by my chosen attire for this evening: a tank top and a pair of boy short underwear.

"Why?"

"Because that's what people do."

"Yes, but—"

"You've been trying to extend an olive branch, and I was just offering to watch television. Nothing more, nothing less."

"What's the catch?"

"I get to choose what we watch?"

That made Nash chuckle and I considered it a small victory.

I could tell that he was still suspicious. He only started to relax when I sat down and curled my body toward him. I reached over and grabbed the remote before settling on a romantic comedy. I saw Nash shake his head out of the corner of my eye, but he did nothing but throw his arm around my waist and pull me closer to him. I'd always enjoyed the feeling of being in his arms. Something as simple as us watching a movie were some of the best memories that I had from when we were dating the first time around.

His finger dragged along the line of my waistband, leaving goose bumps in its wake. I shivered at his touch and wondered how he'd made me want him again just with a simple graze of his finger.

His thoughts must have been on the same track as mine because his finger dipped below my waistband and began playing with the skin just beneath. After about a minute of his teasing, I'd had enough.

I looked at him and placed my fingers on his jaw. I turned his head so that he was facing me and kissed him passionately.

When we broke apart, he smirked against my lips. "I thought you said it would be nothing more?"

"I did but it looks as if your hand had other plans."

"I guess it does have a mind of its own. Lie back."

The way he said it reminded me of our rendezvous on the kitchen counter in his apartment. I could feel the heat climbing in my cheeks as I debated on doing what he said. An idea came to mind, and I realized that I had another trick up my sleeve.

Instead of lying back on the couch, I shifted my body so I could swing my leg over his lap and lower my body onto his. His eyes turned darker, and I didn't know if it was because I disobeyed his order or because I'd turned him on even more.

He tucked a piece of my hair behind my ear before he leaned forward and kissed me. My hands landed on his chest as his fingers anchored my head into place while he devoured my lips. Nash's hands made their way from my face to the straps of my tank top. He slid the straps down my arms and freed my breasts from my shirt. His hands played with my breasts, lightly shaking them before turning to massaging them. He squeezed them slightly before sticking one of my nipples in his mouth.

My head flew back, and I moaned, enjoying the sensations that his tongue was causing in my body. He nibbled on my breasts and licked them to soothe the area. His attention alternated between them for a few moments before I leaned back, moved my hands to cup my tits and mushed them together. He groaned at the sight.

Nash took on the challenge of licking both of my nipples at the same time as I grinded into his lap. I could feel him growing harder and I wanted his dick inside me as soon as possible.

As if he heard my inner thoughts, Nash reached into his pocket and produced a condom.

"You were prepared."

"Whenever I'm around you, I have to be."

I smiled and leaned forward to kiss him again.

I moved my body so he could pull his black sweatpants down and roll the condom down his shaft. When he completed the task, I shifted back on top of him and helped guide his cock into me.

I put my hand on the arm of the couch and began to ride him. His gaze shifted from my face down to my breasts.

"Watching your tits bounce while you're riding my cock is…" His voice trailed off as a moan left his lips. Being able to see him in such a state made me feel even more powerful. I was causing him to behave this way and I loved it.

Love.

It hit me like a ton of bricks. The feelings that I'd had for him that I thought I'd buried months after I left Brentson had come back with a vengeance. I could chalk it up to the amazing sex that we were having but I knew that was a lie. I was in love with him again. Maybe I always had been.

I hadn't expected this to happen but wasn't that what love was all about? I wasn't prepared to say it out loud, but I was in love with Nash Henson. Fuck.

He hadn't given me any indication that he felt the same. Hell, I wasn't even sure if he believed me when it came to the lie that his father told him about me. I pushed those thoughts aside as he began to meet my thrusts with some of his own. It was as if he'd noticed that I'd gotten lost in my thoughts, and this was his attempt to bring me back to him without actually saying so.

"Fuck, baby," he said.

Nash reached up to pinch my nipples, I cried out. Being the one in control of both of our pleasure was a new experience and I wanted to do it again and again and again.

I reached down to touch my clit and he groaned. His hands ended up in my hair and he pulled it back, exposing my neck and providing a new dimension to our fucking. We both sailed off the edge together, and I leaned my forehead on his to catch my breath.

I had to use the arm of the couch to help me steady myself until I was sure that I could walk. Once I fixed my clothes, and he did the same, he also stood up and pulled me flush against his body before laying a searing kiss on my lips.

Together we walked into the bedroom to commence

round two. But there was something that was laying in the pit of my stomach and making me feel like shit.

I knew I needed to come clean, especially now that it seemed like Nash liked me again, but I didn't know when the right time would be. Instead, I adjusted my body, allowing myself to fall deeper into his arms before I went to sleep.

16

RAVEN

The shower felt like paradise. Staying in the middle of the woods in a cabin wasn't my idea of a vacation, nor was hiding from someone who wanted to harm me, but this shower made everything so much better. Or maybe it was because it felt as if things were getting better with Nash.

He hadn't been in bed when I woke up this morning and I chose to take a shower first instead of going to see where he was. I still felt sore in all the right places, and I knew that a shower would do some good in helping my tired, aching muscles. My time under the showerhead gave me an opportunity to think and dissect every problem that I had in my life, yet I wasn't able to draw any answers that would help me solve any of them. Although it was frustrating, I did feel more relaxed as I turned off the water and grabbed my towel.

After pulling myself together, I walked out of the bathroom, into the bedroom, where I grabbed my phone. Then, I continued into the living area where I assumed Nash was. The first thing that hit me as I walked through the doorway was the smell of something delicious. I found Nash walking to the dining room table with dishes in his hands.

He glanced up. "Oh good, You're just in time."

"You had brunch delivered? This is a lot of food, especially for two people."

"No. Well, ninety percent of the things on the table I cooked myself."

"You know how to cook?" The question slipped out of my mouth before my inner filter could stop it.

"I learned from our chef when we were growing up."

To say I was impressed was putting it mildly. I didn't know he'd known how to cook in high school because it never came up. I took some cooking classes here and there to improve my skills while I was away, but I wasn't a professional chef by any means. My mom had instilled a love for food and cooking when I was younger, which came in handy when she had to start working two jobs to make ends meet. Sometimes she would come in, exhausted from work, just as I was putting food on the table and would thank me profusely before shoving the food into her mouth. Sharing dinner with my mom was special given how often I didn't see her.

It was then that I realized I hadn't done much cooking since I'd been back and that needed to change... eventually. Maybe that would be the first thing I'd do once we left the cabin.

I sat down at the table and took in the food before me. Nash had made sure that neither of us would need any more food for a while. Eggs, bacon, pancakes, French toast, and fruit had taken up a large section of the table. Nash placed an empty plate in front of where I usually sat. The fact that I had a usual seat at this dining room table made my eyes almost pop out of my head. This was the location where my ex took me after he kidnapped me, and here I was, treating it like it was a home away from home.

I served myself as Nash asked, "What would you like to drink?"

I froze briefly before I went back to what I was doing. "Orange juice. Thank you."

"No problem."

I waited until he returned to say something else. "Everything smells great, Nash."

"And it'll taste even better."

"Cocky much?"

"It's not cocky if you can back it up."

The look in his eyes told me he was talking about more than just cooking. "That's corny. Even for you."

Nash laughed and I took a sip from my glass of orange juice to hide my grin. We'd definitely fallen back into a rhythm that was similar to what we had in high school, and I wasn't sure how I felt about it.

"When all of this is over, I'm going to take you out on a real date."

"So this is a date?"

He gave me a knowing look but didn't confirm or deny. He didn't need to. I could easily see by the expression on his face that it was what he considered it to be. I bit back the petty remark that I had on the tip of my tongue about how most men didn't have to kidnap women in order to take them out on dates. Our situation was more nuanced than that, but I didn't think I was too far off with my assessment.

I wiped my lips to remove any crumbs. "You mean the dates to Smith's Ice Cream Parlor didn't count?"

Nash chuckled. "Sure they did, but that was years ago now. I'm ready to make some new memories with you."

He actually wanted to go out on a date with me? That confirmed what I'd suspected about the rhythm we'd found again. Since I'd been back, I'd come to terms with the fact that our relationship dynamic consisted of nothing more than our "fuckbuddy due to blackmailing" status. All of our time together consisted of him demanding me to do whatever he wanted, be wherever he wanted. Besides taking me to his parents' party just to piss off his father, we kept those times together well hidden, for obvious reasons. Now, he wanted to take me out like we're an actual couple again? This one-hundred-and-eighty-degree change in direction was something I didn't know if I was ready for.

But at least there was good food for me to enjoy while I overthought every aspect of this brunch.

"Any word on who has been trying to kidnap me?"

"No. I'm going to call around today to see if there are any updates, but no one has reached out to me, unfortunately."

I watched as Nash clenched and unclenched the tablecloth. It was easy to see the frustration on his face. It mirrored what I was also feeling, but there still wasn't much that either of us could do.

"I hope we have an update soon. I can't wait to get back to campus."

"Eager to get away from me?"

The shift in the mood in the room almost made me feel like I had whiplash. I wasn't about to let him get away with it either. "I didn't come here willingly, Nash. You know that. So don't get angry with me when I asked for none of this."

He nodded and ate a piece of his French toast without another word.

It seemed as if he too had fallen victim to the atmosphere we'd built out here. The rockiness that came about as a result of this situation would be difficult to get past. While it had been easy to fall into old habits, even after all of this time, it was easy to fall victim to them. There would be a lot that would need to be done for us to make it past this. That was, if we ever wanted to make it past this.

17

NASH

"There had to be a reason why Paul came after her, Chairman."

I held my phone up to my ear as I looked through the doorway toward the bedroom. The only thing I could see was Raven's feet tapping along to the sound of the music that I knew was coming through my ear pods. She'd asked me for them about ten minutes ago and they were obviously doing their job of making sure that she could get lost in the music. They were also making sure she couldn't hear the conversation I was having with Tomas.

"I know, and while we don't know who sent him, as far as I know, no one else has made an attempt to try to finish the job. By the way, this intel is coming from leadership that is higher than me in the Chevaliers."

That was good news. We needed to head back to Brentson anyway because that was the promise I made to Raven, and while I wasn't one hundred percent confident that she was absolutely safe, the fact that someone else wasn't lurking around trying to pick up where Paul left off was a good sign.

"I'm surprised you were able to get input from Chevaliers that aren't on our campus."

"They tend to take on cases they deem to be... special sometimes."

"What do you mean?"

"I can't go into further detail about it. Just know that, as of now and from what we know, there isn't another credible threat on Raven."

His words should have been reassuring, but how much we didn't know left me feeling insecure.

"Okay. Thank you for asking around about this for me."

"You're welcome. I'll see you on campus soon."

I hung up and turned my attention to heating up dinner for Raven and me. Suddenly my phone vibrated on the kitchen counter. When I saw who was calling, I ran my fingers through my hair before tugging hard on it.

It was my father.

I'd been mostly ignoring him since I started shit at their party and I fully planned on ignoring him now.

Things had been peaceful in the cabin since Raven and I spoke yesterday, and I wanted to keep it that way.

I sent the call to voicemail and just before I could take the food out of the oven, my phone vibrated again.

I bit back a curse. He wasn't going to give up this time, was he?

"Hello."

"Son?"

I rolled my eyes. "What do you want, Dad? So that I can get you off the phone."

"I want you to open the damn door to the cabin."

I froze, not out of fear but out of surprise. I knew it would only be a matter of time before he knew I was here. What I hadn't been expecting was for him to show up. I maybe had a few seconds to warn Raven about what was going to transpire.

I walked into the bedroom where I knew I would find her. She turned to me with a warm grin and removed the ear pods. I dreaded having to take the smile off her face.

"Hey, what's up? Is dinner ready?"

"It almost is, but we have a surprise guest that should be here shortly. My father."

I watched as her smile fell and her face took on a more neutral look. "Why?"

"Who knows? But depending on when he found out I was here, I'm surprised he stayed away this long."

"I'm going to stay in here until he leaves."

"Wait, why?"

Her eyes shifted slightly, and she said, "I don't want to get between you and your father, and you saw the way he reacted when he realized you brought me to the party. I would rather the two of you handled it alone."

I wasn't going to try to force her to have to deal with my father on top of everything else. If I could do this and protect her at the same time, then so be it.

"Okay, if that's what you want to do, then that works for me."

"Thanks," she said.

With that, I left the bedroom, closing the door behind me. I made a promise to myself that if my father attempted to go back there, there would be hell to pay.

As I double checked that none of her things were sitting in the living room or dining room, there was a knock on the door. I was surprised he'd given me that much time to do what I needed to do when he seemed very insistent that I open the door as soon as he said to do so.

I cracked my knuckles in preparation for what I suspected was about to happen. I knew how my father got when he was angry, so this could turn into an all-out screaming match. I wouldn't be surprised because the cool, calm, and collected politician that the public saw could turn into a mean asshole behind closed doors. I opened the cabin's front door and my father tried to push his way inside, not even giving me a chance to greet him.

I held up my hand and he looked down at it before looking back up at me. "Hello, Dad," I said sarcastically.

"Don't fucking 'hello dad' me." He glanced around the room before his eyes landed back on me. "I thought you might have company up here. I also figured that was why you were avoiding talking to me."

I moved out of the way and let him into the cabin before I replied, "And by company, I assume you're talking about Raven."

"You just couldn't stay away, could you? Even after all she did, you just couldn't fucking stay away." It was obvious his anger was increasing every second that he stood in this cabin.

I wouldn't admit it out loud, but I was getting a thrill from having him react this way. "Is that the reason why you came here?"

"That's part of it. I came here because I couldn't believe that the son I raised would be willing to throw away everything that we've built in a blink of an eye to start some shit at a party and then disappear. You left all of your responsibilities at school, football, and the Chevaliers behind to come up here and hide for whatever reason. I didn't fucking raise a coward."

I wondered if he'd heard all of the different excuses I'd told on behalf of me and Raven in my attempts to explain our absences, but it seemed as if he hadn't. Not that I was surprised, my father only cared about what I did for how it reflected on him. Missing school for a few days would have gone unnoticed and I was in the clear with the Chevaliers. That left only football to have drawn any attention. The only reason he had ever cared about football was because my skill at it brought our family more recognition and it made him seem more relatable.

"I wasn't feeling well, and I decided to take some time to recuperate here. Nothing more, nothing less."

"And you just so happened to take this break after you murdered someone at the Chevalier Manor."

Neither one of us flinched at the declaration. I wasn't really surprised he'd heard about that too, but I was more intrigued by him not mentioning why I killed him. Perhaps he didn't know all of the details.

"Yes, that was one of the reasons why I needed a break. I lashed out on someone that I shouldn't have, and I needed some time to think things through."

The lie came out way easier than I thought it would have. I didn't give a shit about Paul. After he attempted to hurt Raven, he's lucky I didn't torture him more before I slit his throat. It would have been nice to fire a few shots into his body, not enough to kill, but more than enough to make him scream in agony for a while. Using the machete to cut off a couple of his fingers for thinking he could touch her with them would have felt pretty good too. Killing him almost felt like I'd let him off too easily.

"Maybe this was a wise decision on your part, especially after you decided to crash what was supposed to be a soft introduction to my run for governor with your ex-girlfriend. Do you realize how much of a distraction that could have caused if I hadn't caught myself? She literally tried to ruin our family and you brought her back into my home."

I folded my arms. "Dad, it wasn't like that."

"Oh, really and you were there when she approached me?"

"No, I wasn't. Everything I know about this incident came from you. Raven wasn't given the time to tell her side of the story."

"So what? Are you believing her over your father?"

His defensiveness was what triggered something in my mind. If what he said was true, his anger could be justified but the gaslighting was a complete other thing. He was getting flustered because I was questioning his story. That just left me questioning him more than ever, but I didn't let him know my trust was wavering. I decided that I would draw his attention to a different aspect of this story.

"Do you want to know the real reason why I brought Raven to the party?"

"Yes, I would like for you to explain yourself, Nash." The sternness in his voice would have scared me as a child, but now I didn't give a fuck.

"The reason why I invited Raven to the party is because I knew it would get your attention."

He took a step toward me. "You wanted my attention, you got it. If you ever try to do something like that again—"

"That's the problem with this situation and ninety-five percent of the other issues in this family. Everything is about what you want to do. About your needs, your wants and to hell with anyone else. You never once asked us how we felt about you running for governor. It doesn't just directly affect you. It affects Mom, it affects Bianca, and it affects me. I don't know if you spoke to Mom or Bianca, but you sure as shit never sat down with me one-on-one or with the family as a whole to talk to us about it and make sure that you had all of us on board."

I paused to stare him down and to see if he had anything to say for himself. When he didn't say anything, I continued, "Do you want to know why? Because you didn't give a fuck. So I showed you what it looks like when I don't care either."

I could see his anger was teetering on the edge, ready to spill over, but it meant nothing to me. I couldn't help but smirk.

"You were able to keep yourself together and not make a fool out of yourself at the party and no one is currently the wiser. Congrats, Dad. This conversation is over. If you'll excuse me, I need to get back to preparing to head back to Brentson."

I reached over and opened the front door. "It was lovely having this chat with you." Sarcasm dripped from every word. I waited for my father to come up with a response, but I was surprised when he didn't.

Instead, he walked through the front door and just as he

was about to leave the doorway, he looked over his shoulder and said, "Nash, I know something else is going on here. I hope you heed my warning and stay away from Raven. It's for your own good, trust me."

With that, he stomped out of the door, and I slammed it behind him.

18

RAVEN

Something within me told me that this was going to be a bad idea. The moment Nash told me that his father was here, I knew. It was not surprising to me that he would put his own thoughts and feelings above those of his children. Van coming here for selfish reasons was a part of how he operated, and I assumed Nash was well aware because he was raised by him.

I didn't know much about Nash's current relationship with his father but based on what I knew from high school and about my interactions with him then, the trajectory of this was straight to hell. Van Henson had only grown more powerful since I'd been gone, or that was what I was able to put together based on what I'd been secretly reading up on since being stuck here.

The Chevalier book had made me want to do a deep dive into anything and everything that I could find out about them. Nash, his father, and his grandfather were all a part of the organization. I'd had a feeling this was the case after finding the older photo in the book.

A pang of guilt hit me in my stomach. I didn't put the ear pods back in like I should have and immediately regretted that decision because I was eavesdropping on the conversation without meaning to. The walls in the cabin must have been relatively thin because I could make out most of what they were saying. It was obvious that things weren't going well, but I stayed seated on the bed, keeping my promise to myself that I wouldn't engage because this wasn't my battle. I could hear that I was one of the topics up for discussion, though.

I'd finally had enough and put the ear pods back in my ears and put some music on to drown out the sound. I read over the text messages that Izzy and I sent to each other.

Me: *I hope we'll be headed back to campus soon.*

Izzy: *I hope so too! We all miss you and thought it was so sweet that Nash volunteered to help you out.*

Yea. Sweet. If you knew what really happened, you'd think he was demented.

Me: *Yeah, it was nice of him.*

Izzy: *And you can tell me everything that happened when you get back here.*

Me: *Izzy, I was sick.*

Izzy: *And now you're better so now's the perfect opportunity for...*

She ended her message with two emojis, a purple eggplant and kitty cat, that made me roll my eyes. It was obvious that she wasn't going to let it go or take a mature stance on this.

I leaned back and closed my eyes. There was no way I was going to be able to attempt to concentrate on another task with what was going on just outside my door. I'd begun to doze off when I heard a door slam. My heart leapt into my throat, the sound causing me to jump because it had been loud enough to be heard through my ear pods with the noise canceling function on.

I assumed that meant Van was gone. When I didn't hear any more loud noises, it seemingly confirmed my suspicions. What it didn't tell me was how Nash was feeling right now. I could assume Nash wasn't happy or pleased. I tapped my foot as I waited to see if he would come into the bedroom to talk about what had just occurred.

But he didn't.

After a couple minutes, I got off the bed and opened the bedroom door. From where I was standing, I saw Nash had his head in his hands. Without a second thought, I walked over to him and placed a hand on his shoulder.

"Is everything all right?"

"Yes, it is."

I expected him to shut down like he'd done before and not elaborate. It took me a moment to mask my surprise when he continued talking.

"I just needed a moment to myself after dealing with him."

"Well, okay. I'll head back into the other room."

As I was about to turn and walk away, Nash's hand shot up and covered mine. The touch of his hand was soothing to me, and I hoped it was the same for him.

"Thank you for checking up on me," he said.

His words warmed me. The entire interaction had been unexpected but very much welcomed. "Of course. I would do it again in a heartbeat."

That earned me a small smile from him. "We're going to leave here in a couple of hours."

I froze. "Wait, we are?"

Nash nodded. "According to my sources, there is no credible threat against you right now. So, we should head back to our normal lives."

To say I was relieved was an understatement. I wanted to get back to my regular routine. I wanted to spend more time with Izzy, Lila, and Erika. Talking to my professors and attending class in person was what I wanted. It felt as if I'd been waiting forever for him to say we could go back, but it did cause a twinge in my heart. We would be headed back to reality soon enough and who knew what lay ahead for...anything.

"This is good news," I said with a hint of a question in my voice.

"It is. It's what you wanted, right?"

I nodded. "Yeah. I want to get back to school and fall back into my life there. If that's what you want to call it."

Nash chuckled. "Well, we can start cleaning up so that we can go."

His hand lingered on mine for a few seconds longer than necessary and a tiny part of me wished he would have just pulled me into his arms. When he let me go, I went to do the things I needed to do to get us out of here in a timely manner. I packed the things that Easton had brought to me, and the things Nash had bought for me while we were here. Once that was complete, I helped Nash clean up the rest of the cabin so that it was in a similar condition to how we found it.

For someone who had money that he could throw away to attempt to fix every problem, I was somewhat surprised he even wanted to bother with cleaning the cabin at all and not just hire someone else to do it. While we were putting things away, he mentioned that a cleaning crew would be coming to clean, but he didn't want to leave them with a huge mess.

We mostly kept to ourselves as we cleared up, and it felt like a blessing and a curse. Not having to talk to him meant that there would be an awkward silence between us. I also could stay lost in my own thoughts much like he seemed to be in his. But it also meant that we were avoiding the elephant in the room.

In terms of his "game," the secret he thought he had on me seemed to be a moot point now. Based on the conversation he had with his dad, he sounded as if he was believing me more and more when it came to his father's accusation.

The other issue that was adjacent to his "game" was I didn't know where this left us. To make matters worse, I wasn't sure what I wanted to happen with us, so maybe it was best that we hadn't spent a whole lot of time talking to one another.

Things between us had started getting better while we were here, but now with our return to campus, I didn't know what this arrangement between the two of us would look like and I couldn't decide what I wanted from him. That, in addition to us not knowing who sent Paul after me, would make me very nervous when I stepped foot onto Brentson University's campus.

19

NASH

"Are you ready to head out?"

Raven looked around the cabin and said, "Let me do one last walk through and I think I should be good to go."

I nodded and found myself staring at her ass as she walked away. The thought of following her into the bedroom after we'd just finished packing and cleaning up did cross my mind. I remained on my best behavior, though, and the glint in Raven's eye when she returned to the front of the cabin told me she wouldn't have minded one bit if I'd done that.

We'd eaten the dinner I was in the middle of heating up when my father arrived in silence. What should have been a relaxing meal turned tense, at least on my end. I didn't know what Raven was thinking, but I'd been still reeling from having to deal with my father.

I grabbed the last bag, letting Raven walk in front of me while I shut the door behind me. I walked with her down the porch stairs to Easton's SUV where I opened the passenger side door for her. She gave me a small smile as she sat down and got comfortable. After I closed the car door, I walked over to the trunk and put the black duffel bag in there and slammed it shut. Once we were both in the SUV, I glanced at her and she gave me another smile, but this time, it didn't quite reach her eyes.

I wanted to ask her what had caused that, but she pulled out her phone and began typing on the screen. Instead of interrupting her, I started the vehicle and began our drive back to Brentson.

When we were on the road, I flipped through the satellite channels until I landed on the soft rock station, allowing that to fill the silence between us. I glanced over at her every so often, but her eyes only drifted between her phone and the scenery out of her window.

I wanted to ask her what she was thinking but trying to force her to talk to me wouldn't work out well.

That meant that the ride back to Brentson was spent listening to music and enjoying the way that the sun set as nighttime began to fall.

As I parked in front of Raven's house, flashes of what happened the night we took off appeared in my mind. It seemed as if the Chevaliers had moved Paul's vehicle somewhere else. Tomas hadn't mentioned it when we spoke, but I appreciated it, nonetheless.

I turned the car off and unbuckled my seatbelt.

"Thank you."

Raven's voice stopped me in my tracks. It was the first time she'd spoken since we left the cabin.

"You're welcome. I'd do it again in a heartbeat." I repeated her words from earlier back to her.

She gave me a small smile before she opened her door. I

hopped out of the car and made it to her side before she closed the SUV's door behind her. The look I gave her made her chuckle. I know she had no issue with opening her own car doors, but when we were dating, it had become a running joke. It was interesting how we fell back into what we did back in high school.

I helped Raven bring her stuff into her house where we found Izzy, Lila, and Erika gathered in front of the television. All three of them stared at us with wide eyes and looked as if they might run toward us, but none of them followed us into her room. I assumed they were giving her space because I was there, but once I was gone, they'd come sprinting in here.

She closed her bedroom door behind me, and we stared at one another, neither one of us saying a word. If we were both on the same page, she also didn't know what to say about the situation we were in. I spent most of the drive going over everything in my mind that had happened over the last week, but the argument with my father stood out the most. How defensive he became. How he didn't seem as angry about Raven being at his party because she supposedly tried to sleep with him to ruin our family, only how it would have made him look in front of his peers if he hadn't been able to keep himself together. None of this was surprising because my father would do anything to protect his image, but this was a new low even for him.

It really hit home for me that I was leaning more toward Raven being the one that was truthful versus my father, which still left the question of what made Raven leave Brentson?

"I'm... not ready to talk about it yet."

I didn't realize I spoke the words out loud until Raven said something. *Fuck.*

"I didn't mean to say that."

She held up a hand and said, "You should know why I left, and I'll tell you soon. I just need to come down off of this adrenaline high I've been on ever since that night."

I nodded. "Well, if you need anything else—"

"I know who to call."

She walked over to me and gave me a long kiss on the lips. I would never complain about kissing Raven, but this almost felt like a goodbye kiss. When we broke apart, I placed my hand on her cheek while I rested my forehead on hers. It was my silent way of telling her this isn't the end.

"I should let you go. I'm sure we have a ton of things to do to get our lives back on track."

"Okay, but I'll see you later," I said the sentence more confidently than I felt. This was the first time in a long time that I was unsure about something in my life. I was always confident when I stepped out onto the football field or throughout what might be pure hell when it came to the Chevalier chairman trials. But Raven's presence had completely thrown me into a direction I never imagined, and I felt as if I was on shaky ground.

"Yeah, I'll see you around."

Together we left her bedroom and I waved to Izzy, Erika, and Lila before we walked to the front door. I opened my arms and she stepped into them for a long hug. It felt more natural than I'd anticipated. I enjoyed having her close to me. The truth was that it had always felt right to have Raven in my arms. I walked away from her and down the front steps to get into my car that was blocking their driveway.

I gave her a small wave right after I started Easton's SUV and then waited for her to close the door before I looked around. I wanted to make sure I didn't see anything suspicious, given what happened the last time I was here.

Seeing nothing, I pulled away from the curb and headed to my apartment.

20

RAVEN

I shifted my book bag that was hanging off my shoulder as I walked into the political science building on Brentson's campus. It was my first day back to this class and I was willing to admit that my nerves were getting the best of me.

These were the same nerves that I felt on my first day of classes at Brentson. It felt weird having to go through this all over again, but it was the added pressure of not knowing if someone else was watching me and if they were, when they would strike again. But at least I made it to class safely.

As I was putting my book bag down at the chair I usually sat in, Dr. McCartney, my professor for this class, looked up at me and smiled.

"Raven, how are you?"

"I'm doing better, Dr. McCartney. Thank you for asking."

The lie fell off my lips easily. It did help that I'd been practicing what I was going to say because people kept asking me. I felt guilty because it was obvious people genuinely cared about me, which was something I hadn't experienced on this scale in a long time.

Dr. McCartney turned to one of my classmates and started speaking to him. I settled into my seat and put my textbook, my phone, and my laptop on my desk. As I was zipping up my bag, I looked up from my desk and out the classroom door and had to do a double take. Landon was standing there. He gave me a slight nod, acknowledging that we'd seen each other before he walked away. It was weirdly unsettling, and I didn't understand what his deal was.

I checked my phone and saw that there was still two minutes before class was set to begin. *Shit.* I tapped my foot as I wondered what I should do. My body moved before I could stop myself. I was on a mission to finally set the record straight with him. I avoided some of my other classmates that were trying to get to their seats and walked quickly to the classroom door and looked in the direction I saw him go in. He was still visible, so I followed him.

"Landon," I called out, but that didn't stop him from walking. Did he have headphones in or something?

"Landon!" I yelled a bit louder as I jogged after him. A few people turned to look at me. I shouldn't have been running if I wanted to keep up appearances about me having been too sick to attend classes for the past week, but at this point, I didn't care what anyone else thought. The determination to get answers had won out over keeping up appearances.

When he didn't respond to me again, my legs went into another gear.

"Landon!"

This time he paused, but he didn't turn around. What the hell was his problem? When I finally caught up with him, he turned around and studied me closely. It was ironic that I went from wanting his attention so that I could talk to him to being freaked out about the attention he was giving me because of how he was staring at me.

He spoke first. "Is there something you need, Raven?"

"Actually, yes I do."

"Well then how can I help you?"

The professional tone he was taking with me was weird, given we didn't meet in a professional environment, but I was willing to ignore it because I needed answers.

"Why does it seem like every time I see you, you're staring at me and then you walk away before I can talk to you?"

"That's very arrogant of you to think that I was staring."

I was taken aback by his statement, but I quickly recovered. "Look, cut the bullshit. What's going on?"

Landon looked to his left before looking back at me. "The only thing I'm going to tell you is that you need to be careful."

This sounded similar to what Nash told me. "What do you mean I need to be careful?"

Landon checked his watch on his wrist. "I mean exactly that. You need to be careful."

"That doesn't help me. You're doing this on purpose."

I could have shaken him or punched him in the face out of frustration. "Just say it! What do you know that I don't?"

"The incident that led to you leaving Brentson this time around? Could easily happen again. Be. Careful."

"But wait—"

Landon didn't bother waiting for me to finish my sentence. He turned to walk away, leaving me wondering if I should try to go after him. Seeing how I left all my things in the classroom, I decided that going back was the best option.

I didn't want to bring more attention to myself, not after having been absent for several days already. I turned around and walked back to class with a newfound determination that this wasn't the end of the conversation with him, and I would get more answers out of Landon the next time I saw him.

I walked back to class and thankfully all of my things were where I left them. I sat down and grabbed my phone off my desk. Texting Izzy just before class started would just have to do.

Me: *Do you have Landon's number or know where he lives?*

It was a longshot based on how big our campus was, but it didn't hurt. I put my phone on vibrate and put the screen facedown. I knew that if I didn't, I would be staring at it for the entire time I was in class.

Thankfully, class flew by, and it felt good to be back. After doing online classes after I left Brentson, I realized that I did better when attending class in person. There was something about being in the room and working that made it easier for me to concentrate. I was actually surprised at how well I'd been able to focus today because what Landon had said was playing on repeat in my mind. Was he somehow connected to Paul? I needed to tell Nash.

I quickly packed all of my things and then picked up my phone. The first thing I saw was a text notification from Izzy.

Izzy: *I don't have any contact information on him. But maybe his contact information is in the directory? Brentson sends one out at the beginning of each year.*

Me: *Do we have one in the house?*

While I waited for her to respond, I walked to my car, making sure to look around for Landon, just in case he was hanging around. Of course, because I was looking for him, he wasn't.

Izzy didn't respond before I got in and started my car, so I drove home and parked in the driveway. I strolled into the house and found her in the kitchen.

"Oh, shit, I forgot to respond to your text. I don't think we have a directory in the house...I'm not sure if it's online."

"That seems like a breach of privacy."

Izzy shrugged. "Take it up with the higher ups. What's up with the sudden interest in Landon?"

I decided that I wouldn't tell a complete lie. "I ran into him today, but he was acting weird, so I wanted to make sure he was okay."

"That's kind of you."

I dropped my book bag near my feet and folded my arms across my chest. My lip twitched as I said, "Was that sarcasm?"

"No I was—" Izzy's eyes widened briefly before she saw the look on my face. Then she glared at me. "Stop fucking with me."

I chuckled. "Yeah, maybe I will, but I'm really not sure what's up with him."

"Hopefully, it's nothing serious."

But it was something serious if it had to do with my safety. My phone vibrated in my back pocket. I fished out my phone and smiled. It was a text from Nash.

"It's him, isn't it?"

That forced me to look at Izzy. "Him?"

"Nash. That's the only reason you usually have that silly grin on your face since you've been home."

"You've seen me twice since I've been back home."

Izzy's eyes narrowed. "Yeah, and either he was with you, or he texted you. I'm willing to bet...our next round of drinks, whenever that will be, that it's Nash. You're paying."

I rolled my eyes, and she threw her hands in the air as if she'd just won a million dollars. I leaned down to grab my bag.

"I fucking knew it! Tell him I said hello!"

I waved her off as I headed into my room. I closed my bedroom door behind me, tossed my bag near my desk, and belly flopped onto the bed before bringing my phone up to my face so I could read the text message.

Nash: *Come to my game this weekend.*

He left no way for me to argue with him in his text.

Me: *If you want me to.*

Nash: *I wouldn't have said so if I didn't. It'll be like old times.*

I thought back to the times I used to attend his football games in high school. Somehow, I suspected that while it might be like old times, it would be on a much different and bigger scale.

Me: *Haha yes it will.*

The laughter that I was trying to portray was nowhere to be found. Whenever he referred to the times when we were together in the past, it threw me into a spiral about what life could have been like if I'd stayed. I didn't wait for him to respond before I sent him a text back.

Me: *I need to talk to you about something important.*

I thought he would text me back, but instead he called.

"Hello?"

"It's so good to hear your voice. You know it reminds me of the sounds you make when I—"

"Nash, are you in public?"

He chuckled. "So what if I am? I'm talking low enough so that no one can hear me."

"You're ridiculous." He sounded cheerful, the happiest that he's sounded since we got back in touch.

"Wouldn't be the first time I heard that. What did you need to talk to me about?"

"It's about Landon."

The pause on the other end of the line made the butterflies in my stomach flutter and not in a good way.

"What about Landon? Have you been in contact with him recently?"

Was that...jealousy? "Yes, but not in the way you're thinking."

"In what way am I thinking, Little Bird?"

The way he said my nickname usually would have made me swoon, but this time was very different. His voice had a dangerous edge to it, one that part of me wanted to run away from and the other part of me wanted to explore.

"He's not trying to fuck me or anything."

"Oh, well that's a relief."

"There's no need for you to be sarcastic right now."

I heard him sigh before he spoke again. "I apologize. What did he do?"

I bit the corner of my lip as I wondered if there was anything I should hold back from Nash. I shook my head. If Nash was really all about protecting me, I should tell him. It might be a mistake, but I didn't have much to go on outside of this. "Whenever I've run into him recently, he had been staring me down. Didn't approach me, didn't say hi. Just stared me down. Not just today either. He was doing it before... well, before you and I went away last week. I saw him staring from the hallway before my last class today, so I chased him down and talked to him briefly.”

“And what did he say?”

“He told me to be careful. He said that the incident that led me to leave Brentson this time around could happen again. I assumed he was talking about me leaving with you.”

“Interesting.”

“Now, Nash, I don’t want you to do anything to him. Like hurt him or—”

“Kill him?” He finished my sentence, and this time, I wasn’t pissed that he had.

“Yeah.”

“Well, I’m going to talk to him about it anyway. Don’t worry about it and if you need anything else, call me.”

“You know where he is?”

He waited a beat before he responded. “I have a damn good idea where he might be. I’ll call you back. But if you get the feeling that something is up, I want you to call me. Got it?”

I nodded even though he couldn’t see me. “I will. Promise.”

“Okay. I—” He paused as if he was about to say something more, but he caught himself. “I’ll talk to you later.”

“Okay. Goodbye, Nash.”

I ended the call and fear kicked in. What the hell had I just gotten Nash into?

21

NASH

I wondered what would happen when Raven and I weren't able to see each other on a regular basis since we were back on campus. I was worried that the progress we'd made toward our relationship while at the cabin was slowly deteriorating. But it looked as if my worry was for naught. Talking to her on the phone reinvigorated me. Well, that and the fact that I needed to find Landon as soon as possible.

I was walking toward Chevalier Manor when Raven called me so I slowed down to take her call. Now that she was off the phone, I opened the front door of the house and walked in.

There was no doubt in my mind that I would find Landon here. After all, we'd been called here to have a meeting about what the schedule would look like for the next series of tasks we needed to complete.

I was happy that I'd arrived in our meeting room early because that gave me an opportunity to talk to Landon if he, too, had arrived early. I sat down in the chair I usually sat in

when we had smaller, more intimate meetings in the confer-
ence room and pulled out my phone to have something to do
until everyone else entered the room.

I read over the texts I'd gotten from Raven and was able to
confirm one of the things my father said when he ambushed
me at the cabin. I couldn't stay away from Raven even if I'd
tried. I was drawn to her, and I couldn't resist the pull.

Although I'd gotten over my anger with her before my
father's visit, it hit me hard after he left, just how much she
meant to me again. You would have thought the rage I felt
toward Paul for what he'd done to her would have been what
made all of that click into place, but it took my father spelling
it out for me to realize it. That was probably the only reason I
would thank him for coming out to see me.

Since we'd returned to campus, I realized why it hurt so
much when she left without a trace. It was because I knew
back then that she was it for me. I didn't want women who
would fall over themselves to replace my coffee or someone
who was willing to try to sneak past Oscar to get into my
apartment. I just needed her. And that was why I was willing
to do anything to protect her. Any-fucking-thing.

I checked the time and noticed that it was five minutes
to the hour. As if that was a sign, Tomas walked into the
room and dipped his head at me, acknowledging my presence. Over the course of the next four minutes, almost all
of the remaining candidates for chairman filed into the
room. The only one missing was Landon, which would be
just my damn luck. Had he dropped out and we hadn't
been informed? Would Tomas make an announcement
here?

Tomas stood up to speak and Landon slipped into the

room, making it to the meeting on time by the barest of margins. He sat down in a chair closest to the door.

"Good of you to join us, Brennan."

"Sorry, I was delayed by a meeting I had just before this."

Tomas stared at Landon for a second more before turning to the rest of us. "Now that we're all here, let's get started."

Tomas looked at each of us before he said, "Congratulations. The reason why each of you are in this room is because you exhibited qualities of an Eagle. Your next tasks will be to showcase qualities that would represent Sparrows and then we will be moving on to Owls. The tasks will start back up again today..."

Tomas's voice faded from my consciousness as I looked over at Landon. He was busy writing something down in a notebook and I wished that I could see what it was.

"Henson."

My attention was drawn back to Tomas who was standing at the front of the room.

"Whatever is distracting you right now, forget it, or I'll have to dismiss you. This isn't a game."

I raised an eyebrow at him. I didn't appreciate being talked to like a child, but he was right that I had been distracted. As I debated responding, a couple of the other guys in the room snickered. If he was alluding to my playing football, then that was clever, and I would give him that. I decided against saying anything because I didn't want to make this a bigger deal than it needed to be. Plus, I needed him on my side in order to reach my ultimate goal.

We weren't given any hints about what the next tasks would be, but I'd been hoping that the next tasks wouldn't be anytime soon. I wanted to have time to figure out who was trying to harm Raven without having to worry about the tasks for the chairmanship and football, but it looked as if I wouldn't have that luck. Without a doubt, I was royally fucked.

I knew that our next task or two would have us showcasing the qualities that had been found in those that became Sparrows. Their focus had been on being hardworking and caring. I was an Eagle, because of my loyalty to the Chevaliers and my strength. I already had an advantage because I easily made it through the obstacle course and showed loyalty through killing Raven's kidnapper. How that went in terms of showing the Chevaliers that I was well on the way to conquering her, since they thought she was my greatest weakness, was a different matter. And I might never have the answer to that.

Owls were known for being wise so I could only imagine what bullshit they might throw at us for that.

Not telling us what we were in for was a way to keep us on our toes and to force us to be prepared for anything. I knew that I was ready for whatever they would throw at me under normal circumstances, but with Raven thrown into the mix, I didn't know what to expect. Which was further proof that it was smart of them to list her as the person I needed to conquer.

Tomas turned away from me and announced, "Power. It's something you all crave. After all, you wouldn't be vying to try to become the next chairman if you didn't want the power of that position. But once that power is in the wrong hands, it could be detrimental. Which is why we have these trials. I want to remind each of you of that as we move on."

I had really hoped that I wouldn't have any tasks to do

over the coming days but suspected I wouldn't be so lucky. That was one of the reasons I asked Raven to my football game this weekend. I had a feeling that after the game would be the only time that I would have free, and that would be the best way to see her.

First, I needed to find out what the hell Landon was up to. Second, I needed to get through whatever they were going to throw at me.

But for now, I was going to focus on what Tomas was saying and contemplate what my next move was going to be.

"DOES ANYONE HAVE ANY QUESTIONS?"

Tomas's question seemed to vibrate off the walls due to the silence in the room. Everyone chose to shake their heads instead of answering out loud, I assumed from caution. None of us wanted to make the wrong move and jeopardize what we'd been working for.

"You are dismissed. I'll see you back in this room in a little over an hour."

Out of the corner of my eye, I saw Landon stand up first. He might try to get away from me, but there was no way I was going to let that happen. I wanted answers and I wanted them now.

It took some maneuvering since Landon left the meeting room first, but I quickly caught up with him and threw my arm around his shoulder.

"Looks like you and I need to have a chat."

He shrugged his shoulder to shake my arm off and said, "I

don't know what we'd have to talk about. We don't have much in common."

"See, that's where you're wrong. We do have one particular person in common and I warned you to stay away from her. But you can't seem to, which I don't understand. And that's not putting into consideration the fact that you were staring me down after I got off the bus when I was coming back from an away game. So, I think we need to find somewhere private where we can... chat."

With a heavy sigh, Landon said, "Come on. We can go up to my room."

I hadn't paid much attention because I didn't realize that Landon still lived in Chevalier Manor. I'd opted out of it once I had the opportunity to do so and I thought that most juniors and seniors did, so I thought it was interesting that he hadn't.

We didn't speak until he closed his bedroom door behind me.

I wasted no time getting to the heart of this encounter. "Why did you tell Raven today that she needed to be careful?"

"Because she should be. It's a dangerous world—"

I was tired and my patience was thin. I had no plans when I came in here of shoving him up against a wall, but it was funny how things changed. "Save me the bullshit, Landon. What information do you have? You knew she left campus and that it wasn't because she was sick. So what have you found out or are you the one who is the threat against her? And I will have no problem taking you the fuck out if you are."

This time, there wasn't a sliver of fear in Landon's eyes.

"What I said was all that I had. Raven needs to be careful because, although you killed her kidnapper, this isn't the end of it."

"The end of what?"

"They are going to keep coming for her, until they reach their goal."

"Who the fuck is they, and what is their goal? Stop talking in riddles."

"I'm not talking in riddles. I'm telling you everything I can because I don't know who they are either."

I tightened my hold on him. "Then how did you find any of this information?"

"Well, I'm not allowed to disclose that information because it would jeopardize everything."

22

NASH

"What did he tell you?"

Raven didn't waste any time saying hello.

I ran a hand through my hair. "Nothing more than you know, but I want you to be extremely careful. Make sure you aren't alone if you can avoid it, but that's all he was willing to tell me."

"Do you think he knows more?"

"I threatened him, and he knew that I would carry it out. Still said the same thing. I have a better suggestion. You can move in with me and I have a doorman that will—"

"Um..."

Raven's hesitation made me stop. The words had flown out of my mouth before I could catch them.

"The other option would be for me to drop the things I'm doing and—"

"Negative on either option, Nash. I'll be sure to try to not be alone until we know whoever is doing this. I don't want you to feel as if your life is on pause because of me."

"I'm trying to protect you."

"And I know that. But you need to play football, you need to do what you need to do for the Chevaliers, and you need to—"

"What do you mean I need to do for the Chevaliers? What do you think you know about them?"

I heard her mumble the word *shit*. She let out a deep sigh before she said, "I read a book in the cabin that I think belonged to your grandfather."

I could almost bet I knew what book she was talking about. He had a few books on the Chevaliers, but one had been missing the last time I went up to the cabin and I hadn't been able to find it.

"I found a photo of you, him, and Bianca in it."

Bingo. "Why didn't you tell me?"

"I was upset with you at the time, and I didn't want to talk to you. I also figured telling you would increase the anger that was between us, so I kept it to myself. It was the evening you ordered Smith's ice cream."

"Fair enough."

"You're not mad?"

"No, but you should have told me." There was no reason for me to get pissed. The book contained some pretty basic information about the Chevaliers and some of our most prominent members. But nothing relating to our rituals should have been in there so that meant that Raven was safe. Because if she had learned some of our major secrets without being a member, then... there was more than likely nothing I could do to save her. That was one of the things we signed up for when we became Chevaliers.

"I should have. I apologize."

I pulled the phone away from my face and looked at the

time. "I have to go but stay with your roommates and we can discuss further arrangements."

"Nash, I'm a grown woman and can do what I want. I told you what I'm going to do and that's it. Now, I'll see you at your game on Saturday."

She hung up on me. If I didn't have to do the next chairmanship task, I would be going over to her house right now to spank her ass, without question.

The time between the meeting with Tomas and the next task was barely an hour and my time was cut shorter because of my run in with Landon. I'd walked out to my car so I could talk to Raven in private. I didn't know who might be listening in, especially since Landon knew the real reason why Raven and I were gone for several days. Now, I might have had just enough time to grab a small snack, but that was it.

It was go time.

The Chevalier Manor had their own chef and staff, so the kitchen was always fully stocked. That made it easy to grab a couple of bags of chips and refill one of my water bottles. I had eaten lunch, but I wanted to eat something now because I didn't know when my next meal was coming.

I scarfed down the snacks and drank my water before joining everyone back in the meeting room. I watched as Landon sat down, once again near the door, and when our eyes met, he nodded at me. Tomas was the last to join us.

"So I'm sure that all of you are wondering what your task for tonight is going to be."

I nodded but couldn't tell if the guys in the room were nodding as well.

"Tonight, you're going to be working in teams of two and

helping to narrow down our next class of initiates into the Chevaliers."

I groaned inwardly. I worked better when I was solo. I only hoped that I would be lucky enough to get paired up with any guy in the room besides Landon.

LUCK WASN'T on my side because, of course, I'd been paired up with Landon to help guide a few men through the next steps they needed to take in order to become Chevaliers. Although this encompassed the friendly nature of the Sparrows, this was the last thing I was thinking this task might be. I didn't realize that part of my job would be to babysit freshmen and sophomores.

At least they were so scared that they didn't want to talk, and they had every right to be frightened. They weren't in any way, shape, or form prepared for what was about to go down, because there was no way that you could be. They'd all already passed the screening phase to become a Chevalier and now they were in the process of becoming members. But nothing could prepare them for what they were about to see and do.

The lights in the room were turned low and Landon and I were in our cloaks, shrouding us almost completely in mystery. It felt weird being on the other side of this ritual, but I recognized it for the honor that it was.

Even with the lights down, I could see one of the guys standing near me was nervous. That wouldn't do.

I leaned down and said, "You alright there, man?"

He nodded quickly but didn't say a word.

"What's your name?"

"Josh." There was a slight tremble in his voice, confirming my suspicions about him being nervous.

"Listen, Josh. It's okay to be nervous or afraid. We all were in your position once upon a time, but what you can't do is give up. Got it?"

He nodded, and I stood up and went back to my position. I didn't want to coddle him, but I knew he would be in for some shit when he found out what their next task for initiation into the Chevaliers was going to be.

They were going to find out that they would have two days to provide a sacrifice to our chairman and leadership board, and if you wanted to back out then, it was too late. You were already in far too deep, and the result would be the end of your life.

That's at least what happened to one of the guys who should have been in the initiation class after mine. Caleb Johansen. In public, it was an accidental situation and that was the information that was told to his parents. In reality, he refused to comply with this task. Rumors flew around about the reason why he died and if it was in connection to us, but nothing was confirmed.

But every Chevalier on campus knew what really happened. It was sad because it could have been avoided.

I remembered my sacrifice like it was yesterday. Shock vibrated through the room when we were told what we needed to do, and I immediately rose to the occasion. There had been no hesitation on my end and the thrill that resulted could never be replicated any other way.

Because that wasn't even my first kill.

23

NASH

"**S**on, you know what you have to do."

I glanced at my dad before looking back at the situation that was unfolding before me. The man before me was bleeding from his mouth and nose after being pummeled by my father. I had no idea what his name was or where he came from. He spit out blood and what looked to be a tooth before grunting. How I'd gone from procrastinating my chemistry homework by chilling in my bedroom and texting this girl from class to taking part in this was anyone's guess.

It started off with my father knocking on my door, telling me that we had somewhere we needed to be and us ending up in a seemingly abandoned warehouse. Everything else happened so fast it was a blur. It all felt surreal.

"No, I don't, Dad. I'm not sure why I'm even here."

"You're here to learn something. About who you are and what you're going to become."

His words did nothing to clarify why I was here. "I still don't understand."

"There is a lot that you won't know until it is deemed that you *have a right to know, but I will prepare you for it because you're my child." He paused and looked at the man wheezing on the floor like he was worthless to him. "You're going to kill this man tonight."*

My eyes widened slightly, and I waited to see if my father was kidding. When there was no punchline after what he'd said, I knew he was serious. Dead serious.

"But why?"

"He fucked over several people, including myself. Now he has to pay for his actions. And I thought I would pass on the honor to you."

The guy laying at my feet looked pitiful, but I couldn't kill him. It was inhumane. I couldn't believe my father expected me to do this. That didn't mean that I hadn't seen or heard some of the things that he'd done when he thought that I was sleeping. Just that I thought he'd quieted down on these types of antics because he was now mayor of Brentson. I assumed he wanted to keep any signs of controversy away from him because it might harm the goals he wanted to achieve. Clearly, I was wrong.

"I don't want to do this, Dad."

"This fucker here tried to rob our family. He tried to swindle millions from us in some fucked up Ponzi scheme and do you know where that would have left us if I hadn't found out in time? Destitute."

I highly doubted we would have been destitute since the Henson family fortune was worth billions. How it had been acquired probably didn't make us much different than the man on the floor trying to wipe the blood from his face.

But having him try to steal from us did completely change things.

My father walked around his body, taking inventory of the damage that had been done before kicking him in the stomach as hard as he could. The man doubled over, forgetting about the blood coming from his face, instead choosing to hold his stomach. It took him a bit to catch his breath and he looked up at me before turning his head to look at my father.

"You're not going to get your kid to do something you aren't man enough to do, Van, are you?"

My father shrugged and I knew why.

I had to admit, this guy clearly didn't give a damn. He wasn't attempting to beg my father to stop or to spare his life. He truly didn't care what happened and had no issue with egging Van Henson on. Even I knew that was a huge error in judgment. All it would do was further annoy my father, but it wouldn't anger him nearly as much as if he'd tried to destroy the image that Van Henson had spent years cultivating.

The bloodied guy on the floor turned and looked at me again. "Do you have more courage than your old man here? Are you going to start doing his dirty work now?"

"Nash, do as I said so we can get out of here."

"I don't feel comfortable doing it."

"It's your first time. I don't expect you to be absolutely comfortable, but there will be a time in your life when this will come in handy. Do it so that we can head home before dinner is served."

I took a step toward the man on the floor. He gave me a wide grin and I could clearly see that he was missing a tooth. I stepped over his body and pulled his head back before reaching out to grab the knife from my father. When he placed it in my hand, I felt a power that I'd never felt before. I was in control of whether this man lived or died.

Men walked out of the shadows, and I hadn't even realized they were there. Their arrival sparked an immediate change in the man's behavior. He was finally afraid, and he started screaming, not that it would help. My victim continued to scream even though I'd slit his throat, but before I could do anything else, my father handed me a towel and turned me away.

"Next time, stab right here," he said as he gestured to a place on his neck. "It silences them quicker that way."

I nodded and continued walking with him by my side.

My father put his arm around me, and I was taken aback. He then said, "But what I should have said first is good job, son."

I refused to acknowledge him because of what he'd convinced me to do. Instead, I checked my phone and noticed that I'd had a text notification.

Raven: I'd love to go out with you. Just let me know the place and time.

She'd ended her text with a smiling emoji. It was the perfect end to a thrilling night.

"YOU KNOW what you need to do! Fucking do it!" Tomas's yell surrounded us, easily letting everyone know who was in charge of this scenario. It was two days later, and time for our next ritual.

These scared, soon-to-be-initiates were standing before the sacrifices who were tied to chairs. They had their pick of weapons to choose from and for some reason, I kept a closer eye on Josh as the ritual continued. Thank fuck I did, because the scene that unfolded before me happened quicker than I could blink.

The guy Josh brought in as his sacrifice got loose and tackled Josh to the ground, flinging the knife he'd chosen to use out of his hand. It was a miracle that neither one of them had gotten stabbed.

I acted on pure instinct. I rushed over to where Josh was being hit and yanked the guy off of him. Before Josh's sacrifice could recover, I punched him in the face.

"This is your kill. You can fucking do it. Here, take this."

Josh wouldn't end up like Caleb. I saw something in him during our brief interaction that told me that he wouldn't have an issue carrying out the task at hand. We wouldn't have to pull together some bullshit cover up story to hide the fact that Josh had become a sacrifice himself in order to prevent a leak about what we really did as Chevaliers. Caleb had done those things which was why he wasn't alive right now.

I gave Josh the knife that he'd been holding before he had been tackled. He took it with a shaky hand, and I gave him a small nod. With my reassurance, he slit his sacrifice's neck. Blood spewed everywhere, but it didn't kill him immediately. His screams could be heard all around us until I snatched the knife from Josh. I stabbed him in the neck where I knew it would both silence him and kill him, and I smirked as I watched his lifeless body fall to the ground.

I looked at Tomas, whose eyes were on me. He nodded at me before I turned and walked away. If that didn't count as me having the qualities of a Sparrow, I didn't know what would.

24

RAVEN

"Are you almost ready?"

I looked up and found Izzy leaning on my bedroom's doorframe with her hands behind her back. She had a huge grin on her face. Her outfit had been perfectly selected and her makeup was done to represent Brentson University. If this wasn't an example of school pride, I didn't know what was.

"I am."

"Something came for you. This was delivered to the house a few minutes ago." Izzy handed me a white gift bag that had white and gold gift paper coming out of it. It matched what she had on, if I was being honest.

I rubbed my hands on my jeans before reaching for the bag. "What the hell is—"

I pulled out the package and found myself staring at a white football jersey with gold lettering. It had Henson on the back and a large number fourteen.

"He can't be serious."

"He loves you. He never stopped loving you."

I rolled my eyes. "Cut it out, Izzy."

"I'm just telling the truth. He went out of his way to make sure you had it. And you dropped this."

Izzy bent down to pick something up off the floor. She handed me an envelope and inside I found two tickets and a handwritten note. She snatched the tickets out of my hand before I could react. Erika and Lila had other plans and couldn't make it to the game.

"These are fantastic seats! Now tell me again he doesn't care about you."

"Izzy..." I was trying to warn her to drop it, but of course she ignored me.

"I don't want to hear it," she said in a singsong voice.

"Then leave so I can finish getting ready and then we can ride the bus over to the field. I don't want to have to deal with parking if we can avoid it."

"Fine. But hurry if that's what you want to do. I'll meet you out front in a couple of minutes."

With that, she left my room. I pulled out the note and quickly read it.

Little Bird,

Maybe next time you'll choose to be in my private suite? Still, being with the crowd is an amazing experience and it will be everything you hoped it would be and more. Meet me after the game near the locker rooms.

N

My cheeks warmed as I read the note again before I realized I was wasting time. I was left running to my closet to find something else I could wear so I could still remain warm but also look great with the jersey on. I found a slim-fit white hoodie that would look good underneath the jersey, and once

I had it on, I stared at myself in the mirror one too many times before grabbing my purse and the tickets. I took another quick glance before walking out of my room and to the front door where Izzy was waiting for me.

We walked outside and saw that the bus was about two blocks away from the closest bus stop to us. Izzy and I jogged over to the bus stop and made it just in time for the bus to pick us up.

We made it to the stadium in good time and it was already starting to fill up. I watched as Nash warmed up.

I could now understand why people were so obsessed with attending college football games. It reminded me of the times I attended Brentson High's games to support Nash, but this was on a completely different level. A sea of gold and white was on complete display and I'd never seen so much school pride at one event in my life.

The rush from being here was electrifying.

"You're Nash's girl?"

Izzy and I turned and found a guy standing over my shoulder.

"Uh..." I was shocked that anyone referred to me as such. I knew that he'd told at least one person that we were dating again, but we'd agreed that we wouldn't need to worry about that when we returned to campus. *Strange.*

"Yes, she is," Izzy said, answering for me.

"He wanted me to let you know that anything you ordered here would be—"

"I can take it from here."

All three of us turned and found Bianca grinning as she walked down the stairs toward us.

"Nash told me that you wanted to sit with the crowd so I

figured I could keep you both company down here. What he was going to say is that anything you order, make sure to mention that you're with Nash and it will be charged to him. But since I'm here, we can make sure that's no trouble." She then turned to the guy that she'd interrupted. "Thanks, Dave. And tell my brother he better kick ass down there."

"Will do."

"I'll be nicer than Bianca and wish him good luck," I said.

"Ditto," Izzy chimed in.

Dave walked back down to the field and Bianca, Izzy, and I were left waiting for the game to begin.

When kick off occurred and the game began, things got wild fast.

Having your ex-boyfriend who you were "fake dating" but for real fucking throw another touchdown pass did certain things to your body. Who knew? I surely didn't until just now. Might be another kink that I'd discovered because of Nash.

"Let's go, Bears!"

Both Bianca and Izzy turned to look at me before laughing. "I didn't expect you to get into this."

School spirit wasn't really my thing, but I couldn't help but be excited for Nash. He was doing amazing, but I wasn't shocked by that, if I had to be honest.

"Raven?"

I leaned over so that Bianca could whisper in my ear.

"Nash mentioned that he wanted you to meet him after the game, so I'll take you down there and then I'll drive Izzy home."

My mouth dropped open and I turned to look at her. "Are you okay with that?"

"Sure. It's not an issue. My brother will owe me, but that's the norm around here."

I laughed and turned my attention back to the game. The anticipation began to build, and I couldn't wait to see what else Nash would do on the field and to see him after it was all over.

I'd been yelling so much throughout the game that my voice began to grow hoarse, which was hilarious to me. Nash's high school games would be exciting, but it was nothing compared to what I'd just experienced. The Bears won their game by over twenty points, and I knew that everyone would be celebrating hard very soon.

We waited about a half an hour after the game was over before Bianca brought me and Izzy down into the stadium and then left me to head back to campus with Izzy.

I spotted Nash first, but he spoke before I could. "There you are."

He pulled me around to a quiet corner and dragged me into his arms and we just stood there, embracing each other as if nothing else in the world mattered. He was freshly showered, and the smell of his shower gel took over my senses. It had a calming effect on me.

"Are you sharing the goods or what? It could be like last time—"

"Brody..." That was the only warning that I had that something was about to happen.

Nash acted before Brody could finish his sentence. A short scream left my lips as Nash slammed Brody against the wall and that was when I realized how powerful Nash really was. It was obvious based on how hard he'd shoved Brody that he could have easily slammed me against the wall in the library's stairwell the first time we spoke again in two years, but he hadn't.

"Nash," I said, but he didn't change his stance.

I put my hand on his before he could do anything he might regret later. He looked like he would have no problem killing this guy right now, and I knew I needed to put an end to this before it came to punches at least. The last thing we needed was for someone to see this that would speak to the press.

"Nash."

This time I was able to draw his attention away from his friend and teammate so that he was focused on me. "This isn't worth it. He isn't worth potentially ruining your future."

What I was saying was true, but it did ignore the fact that his parents would make sure that his reputation was bullet-proof and could survive almost anything. They would make sure of it.

Nash let Brody go and Brody immediately put his arms up.

"I didn't mean anything by it, it was just something that we've done in the past."

"Things change."

"Obviously, I missed the memo. I'll see you later tonight."

Brody left Nash and me standing behind him. I was left wondering just how much things had really changed from when they were into "sharing the goods". Nash shook his head and grabbed my hand.

"You were into sharing women?" I asked as we walked together.

"Emphasis on *was*."

"Are you sleeping with anyone else now?" The question

flew out of my mouth. I'd thought he hadn't been but our experience with Brody made me question it. It's a question we should have approached when this whole thing with us started up again, but at least we were doing it now.

"No. And I'm completely clean if you're worried about that as well. Got tested just before the school year started."

I expected a smart-ass response from him but I was glad that he'd taken my question seriously. "I'm clean too. Got tested two months ago and haven't been with anyone in that time."

Nash nodded as he led me to his car and while it took some time, we eventually made it to his apartment. When he opened the door, I walked in and dropped my purse on the counter before turning to face him.

He closed the door behind him and turned toward me before smirking and said, "It felt amazing having you out there, cheering my name."

"You couldn't hear me."

"Still, I know you were doing it. Listen to your voice."

I rolled my eyes. "I was so amped. I still am. That was such an exciting game. You know what I'm thinking now?"

"What's that?"

I took a step toward him, closing the gap between us. I placed one hand on his chest. The other I used to grab his duffel bag and remove it from his shoulder. It dropped to the floor, and I nudged it out the way with my foot.

"I think it's time for a celebration. Do you remember the last time we celebrated?" The dark look in his blue eyes told me he had. "I thought we could do something like that but a little differently this time."

He turned his body so that he was leaning on the counter.

I dropped to my knees and quickly lowered his sweatpants. I couldn't help but stare at his dick, in preparation for what was about to come. Part of me couldn't believe that I'd voluntarily done this, but I was way too excited from the game.

I grabbed his cock and leaned forward, allowing my tongue to get its first lick. The shiver that traveled through his body at that one motion made me happy. He had no idea what was about to happen to him.

I licked the head of his cock again before taking him in my mouth and sucking on it. I relaxed my jaw and took more of him into my mouth as I looked up at him. Nash was staring down at me and I could see the lust and admiration in his eyes.

"Fuck," he mumbled as he gripped the counter with one hand. I chuckled and he groaned. The vibrations from my laugh must have been his undoing.

I could feel his other hand come up the side of my face, where his fingertips lightly touched my cheek before they made their way into my hair.

"That's right. Take my cock. I'm going to spill all of my cum down that beautiful throat of yours."

I could feel myself growing wetter at his words. His encouragement gave me the courage to take even more of him and I gagged a bit before I pulled back. I massaged his balls, and he sucked in a quick breath.

"Hold still," he said.

I wondered what he was going to do next. My question was soon answered when he moved his hips. He was going to fuck my mouth.

I made sure to hold as still as possible as he plunged into my mouth. His moans and groans grew louder as his pace picked up. His hands made their way to the sides of my face, doing his part to hold my head steady. When his pace slowed, I knew what that meant. Nash pulled back slightly so that he could release his cum into my mouth.

The harshness of his breathing was all I could hear as I swallowed every last drop, making sure to keep the jersey clean. He was trying to catch his breath and I loved the sound of it. Loved knowing I did that to him.

When he was able to calm himself, he said, "That was our private celebration. Let's get cleaned up so we can go party around campus."

25

RAVEN

"Dinner was absolutely delicious, Raven. Thank you."

I grinned at Lila, who'd given me the compliment. My eyes moved from Lila's face to Izzy's, and finally to Erika's and watched as they nodded in agreement. I'd thrown together a lasagna as an early dinner because my roommates had decided to go to a concert that evening. We would have done dinner another night, but it was the only time we were all free at the same time.

I couldn't deny that it felt good to be back in the kitchen and making food and having people love it.

"I'll do dishes," Izzy announced.

"I'll help," Erika volunteered.

"Go. Go relax in your room while we do this." Izzy stood up and shooed me away.

"Okay, okay. I'm going. Let me know if you need me," I said as I stood up from the table.

"We don't!"

I chuckled as I left the kitchen and walked into my

bedroom. After I closed my door behind me, I sat down at my desk and turned on my laptop. I needed to do some research for an assignment even though all I wanted to do was sleep after that heavy meal. I was busy typing on my computer when I heard a knock at my door.

"Raven?"

I looked up from where I'd been working at my desk to see Lila standing at my door. "Yeah?"

"You have a couple pieces of mail waiting for you."

"Wait, really?" I wasn't used to getting mail and now it seemed as if I'd had mail arriving for me daily. It was the day after Nash's football game, but I hadn't checked my mail yesterday.

Something in a tan envelope and an envelope from a sorority? I'm blanking on what the letters mean.

"Ah, okay. Thank you."

I waited for Lila to leave before I tore into the envelope from Psi Delta Mu. I chose to open that piece of mail up first because it caused me less anxiety. I found an invitation for me to join one of their events to get to know the women in the sorority the following week. I thought it was a bit odd that I got invited to such a thing because I figured I wasn't well known on campus outside of the girl who left Nash Henson heartbroken years ago.

Nowhere had I expressed interest in learning more information about a sorority. Things had been too busy with my return to Brentson, and I hadn't thought about joining any activities such as a sorority or clubs. It could be something that I looked into, though.

My hand shook slightly as I picked up the tan envelope. There was no return address. It mirrored the correspondence

I'd gotten just before I got the mail that announced that I'd been accepted into Brentson University. There was no doubt in my mind that it had to be about my mother. I took several deep breaths as I tried to gather the courage I needed to open the letter.

I flipped the envelope over, tore it open, and its contents fell to the floor. I quickly picked up the piece of paper and discovered that it was a newspaper article, but the date had been crossed out. If I had to guess, I would assume it had to be over twenty years old.

There was my mom with a wide smile on her face standing next to three men. The article stated that two of their names were Neil and Martin Cross. I couldn't quite make out the name of the other man in the photo. It seemed to be a fluff piece about how well Cross Industries was doing and it was all thanks to employees like my mother, Clarissa Goodwin.

I read the article again, but I was still confused. Sure, I hadn't known that she worked there, but I didn't know what this was supposed to mean. It was great to find out a piece of her history that I hadn't known before, but what did this have to do with her death? I quickly pulled out my laptop and began researching. Were Neil and Martin part of *the* Cross family, the same Cross family who had a building on Brentson's campus named after a relative? The same family that was mentioned as a prominent member of the Chevaliers?

How far did this all go?

It was much easier to find information on the Cross family than it had been to find information on the Chevaliers. Cross Industries had been created by Virgil Cross, and the family must have donated a lot of money to get one of the main buildings on our campus named after him. Their money seemed to be old and who knew how many businesses they were involved in that went beyond what was reported in the news.

And my mom worked for them at one point.

Were there any clues to this that I missed? Maybe there could be something in my mom's things?

Most of my mom's stuff had been put into storage by the time I left, and I hadn't gone through it since, but maybe it was worthy of a revisit. Nash, Izzy, and a couple of other high school friends had come over to help me pack her things. While it probably made sense for me to have gone through all of her things before they ended up in storage, I couldn't mentally do it and they'd been sitting in there for well over two years now.

Would I be strong enough to do it now?

It didn't matter how hard it might be, this was something I needed to do because it might bring me the answers and closure that I deserved.

I continued going down research rabbit hole after research rabbit hole, trying to find the missing pieces to this puzzle, but I still came up empty. What else could I do to figure out what was going on here?

I glanced at my phone quickly before turning to type another keyword that I hoped would lead me down the right path in my search, but then I paused. If the Cross family and Henson family both had prominent roles in the Chevaliers, was there a chance that they all knew each other?

The timing might be off in terms of when Van Henson and members of the Cross family might have been at

Brentson, they might not have attended at the same time, but they were all a part of the same exclusive secret organization. It would make sense that they would at least know each other as acquaintances.

I grabbed my phone and as soon as I reached the home screen, it vibrated in my hands. The notification showed that it was a text from Nash, as if I'd mentally summoned him.

Nash: *Just finished up some things and I wanted to come over and spend some time with you.*

His text made me grin and I loved it.

Me: *How did you even know that I'm home?*

Nash: *Guessed.*

Or it could have been the text message I sent him earlier today that also included information about how I was going to be alone tonight.

Me: *Well, my roommates are going to a concert about an hour away and I'm going to need someone to stay with me in case danger knocks on my door.*

I was trying to be playful, but I was still worried about what all of this could mean. With the addition of the article that I'd just gotten sent in the mail, it felt as if my thoughts were in a tailspin. I needed a small reprieve before I dove off what would feel like the deep end into whatever this might turn into.

Nash: *Happy to be of service. Sounds like an excellent reason for us to explore your bedroom since we haven't had a chance to fuck in there.*

There was no turning off my grin.

Me: *Game on.*

26

———

RAVEN

My heart skipped a beat for multiple reasons as I watched Nash park his sports car in front of my home. He'd avoided parking near the driveway. I assumed it was done as a way to avoid getting in Lila's way since she was driving Izzy, Erika, and herself to the concert.

I found myself biting the corner of my lip as I watched him step out of the car and couldn't help but admire how fucking hot he looked. It wasn't his clothes, which were in complete contrast to how expensive I knew his car was.

It was all him.

I was beginning to wonder if I was sex starved. But it was more than that.

The news that was sent to me and the secrets I kept were weighing heavy on me. I knew I had to come clean, but right now, all I wanted was him.

I walked to my front door and opened it before Nash even had a chance to knock. He gave me his award-winning smile and I backed away from the door, giving him a chance to step

into the house and not run into me. He tilted his head and I
saw his stare darken.

I held my breath as I walked toward my bedroom. The
quicker I got us out of the shared living space, the quicker we
could get down to what both of us really wanted to do. We
walked into my bedroom and once the door was closed, that
was the end of our stalling.

He turned and pushed me into the wall. It all happened
so fast I thought that my head was going to slam into the wall,
but it didn't. He had placed his hand there to keep it from
happening. Having him standing over me and taking control
was making me more aroused.

Nash tilted my head up and kissed me. His hands drifted
down my body until he was able to pick me up. He broke our
kiss and asked, "Where's your bathroom?"

I stared at him for a moment, still in a daze from his tanta-
lizing kiss and confused by his question. I gestured to the
door to his back. "Just through that other door."

He followed my directions and led us to my bathroom.
Thankfully, I didn't share a bathroom with any of my roommates or we would be giving them a show. He sat me on the
corner of the counter and leaned forward to kiss me again.
His hands reached for my shoulders and shoved my sweatshirt down my arms.

Nash walked away from me and turned the shower on
before walking back toward me, taking off clothes as he did.

"Is this one of your fantasies?"

"Taking a shower with you?"

"Yes."

"I think you know the answer to that."

Yes. A resounding yes.

"Arms up, Raven."

I did as he said, and he took my shirt off with ease.

"You're so fucking beautiful." He said the sentence with so much emotion I wasn't prepared for, and it made the guilt within me build. Instead of focusing on it, I chose to lift my hips slightly so that I could take off my leggings and underwear.

"Did I tell you to take off the rest of your clothes?"

Nash's comment stunned me. "I thought we were heading in there, so I took initiative."

"You're lucky that I want you too fucking bad to punish you for not following my directions."

Before I could react, Nash picked me up again and carefully took me into the shower.

I let the water fall over me without moving, enjoying the way it felt pouring onto my body. I pushed my hair out of my face and opened my eyes.

I found Nash slowly studying my body before he lowered his head down to my ear and said, "Since your roommates haven't left yet, let's see how quiet you can be, Little Bird."

He leaned down and gave me a punishing kiss as the water beat down on us. This shower was nothing in comparison to the one at his apartment, but he didn't seem to mind how much space his body took up in this shower.

As we kissed, my hands ran along his back as I loved the way his muscles felt underneath my touch. His reached down to touch my pussy.

"Put your leg around my waist."

He slid a finger in me, and I gasped. His pace started slow, but quickly picked up. My heart rate sped up and I almost screamed, "I need your cock, now. Fuck me!"

He smirked before his eyes widened slightly. "I forgot a condom."

My heart lurched at not being able to be fucked by him.

"I'm on birth control."

"Excellent. Now put both of your legs around me."

I was moving before he'd finished the sentence. He plunged into me without another word and the feeling was something beyond what I could have ever imagined. He began to fuck me, and before I knew it, there wasn't anything I could do but hold on for dear life. The contrast between the tile at my back, his hot, hard body at my front, and the water that was falling down between us was orgasmic by itself. Having him pound into me this way was almost more than my body could take.

When I felt my orgasm take over, he leaned forward and kissed me, swallowing my cries to avoid us being detected. Then again, at this point, did I really care who knew?

Nash soon joined me on the other side and together we stood there, leaning up against my shower wall, trying to calm down.

"Little Bird, put your back toward me."

I did as he asked, and a moan left my mouth when he placed his hands in my hair and began to massage the shampoo into my scalp. If he would allow me to hire him permanently for this job, I would.

Fantastic sex and then a head massage after? What more could I ask for?

He finished washing my hair and both of us completed our shower. When we were dressed and I put my hair into a long braid down my back, we got into my bed. I found myself laying in Nash's arms and feeling anything but comfortable, but it wasn't because of his body next to mine. Neither one of us said a word, which meant that I was left alone with my thoughts that made me feel nothing but guilt. It was the same feeling I felt at the cabin, and while I'd been able to push back my guilt before, I could no longer do it. I needed to come clean.

I couldn't take it anymore. The article that was dropped off at my house and the secret I'd been keeping felt as if they were killing me slowly. I needed to release the pressure that I'd put on myself.

"Nash."

"Yea?"

"We need to talk."

27

RAVEN

Both Nash and I sat up in bed. Nash walked over to my desk and sat down while I stayed sitting on my bed. "There's a lot you don't know. Some of it I've been keeping to myself for years, other things have just developed over the course of the last couple of days."

"Am I mentally prepared for this?"

I shook my head. "Probably not. But I'm not sure where to begin."

"I always say the beginning, but where you decide to start is up to you."

I put my fingertips to my lips and thought. Did it make sense to start at the beginning? After all, that would probably be one of the biggest bombshells that I told him tonight.

I swallowed hard and realized where I wanted to start, and it wasn't there.

"I got something in the mail today about my mother and it's related to why I came back to Brentson."

"So the reason you came back to Brentson was because of your mother?"

"I-I was promised that I would find out what happened to my mother if I came back here this semester. At first, I thought it was a horrible prank and wondered who would play a disgusting joke on someone who lost the only parent they've ever known so tragically. But then I received this."

I stood up and walked over to where Nash was sitting. I pulled out an envelope that showed my acceptance letter to Brentson and that I was given a full ride to attend.

"I wondered why it had been so easy for you to transfer here. And someone was desperate enough to have you come back here that they paid your tuition in full to get you here."

I nodded. "I hadn't even applied to transfer. It was all done for me, and I thought of it as a sign that I needed to be back here. That, plus finding out exactly what happened to my mother."

I wrapped my arms around myself, and Nash pulled me into his lap. It felt good to have him be here as a source of comfort.

I looked up at him with my tired eyes. "I don't know if you remember this, but I always felt that what happened to my mother was wrapped too tightly in a pretty little bow. I thought there was more to the story, but then wondered if I was being paranoid about the whole thing. After all, it was supposed to be a textbook hit-and-run case and the culprit was never found, so I wondered if I was just holding out hope or if there really was something more there."

"And whoever sent you this, gave you hope."

"Right. And that brings me to what I got in the mail today."

I took out the article that showed a photo of my mother

standing next to three men. I handed it to Nash with a shaky hand.

He studied it and then looked back at me. "Your mother knew the Cross family?"

"Apparently? I don't even know. It says she worked for one of their companies at some point. This has to mean something, but I'm not sure what. It freaked me out regardless, though."

"I... have some connections with the Cross family. I could find out more information if you want me to."

His words were like a Hans Zimmer score to my ears. "You would? Really?"

"Of course I would. If it'll bring you peace of mind and you're okay with whatever I might find, then absolutely."

I thought about it for a moment before I slowly nodded my head. "Yes, I'm ready for whatever you might find out, I think. I'd rather know what happened than not know."

I took a deep breath and chose my next words more carefully. "But you might not want to do anything else for me once you find out my other secret."

"Raven, I—"

"No let me tell you and then you can decide how you feel about it, okay?"

When Nash nodded, I took his approval as a sign to continue. "So now that I told you why I returned to Brentson, I need to tell you why I left."

Nash ran a hand through his hair, and I wondered if he was bracing himself for what I was about to say.

I cleared my throat and continued, "The reason why I left town is because your father paid me to leave."

"He did what?"

Tears were streaming down my face now. Any hope of maintaining my composure had gone out the window.

"He paid me—"

Nash shook his head as if he still wasn't comprehending what I was saying. I couldn't blame him.

"None of this makes any fucking sense. Why would he pay you to leave?"

I swallowed hard before I answered. "Well, it was twofold really. This was something I hoped that I would never have to say to you, but you deserve to know the truth. If it damages what we've started to rebuild, then that's the consequence that I will have to live with for the rest of my life."

I couldn't bear to look at Nash as I told the story. I stood up and began to pace back and forth, trying to figure out how to phrase what I wanted to say. "You know I was going to have a bigger hardship going to Brentson than you because I didn't have money."

Nash nodded. "Of course I knew, we talked about student loans, about you maybe having to take a part-time job. We were exploring any options that could be done so that we could make it work for you to attend."

"Right," I said, but continued to pace. "There was one option that I considered and started the process of going through that I never discussed with you."

"I don't like where this is going," Nash said.

"Trust me. It gets even worse when you finally hear the rest of it." I took a deep breath. "Before I left Brentson, I was in the process of becoming an escort in New York City."

Nash just stared at me but didn't say a word. It was

obvious that the wheels in his head were turning as he tried to process what I'd just said. Although I shouldn't feel guilty about the decision that I'd made as an adult, the look in his eyes made me feel that way.

"You should have told me." He, too, stood up. "How far did it go?"

"Nash, I—"

"How far did it go?" He didn't yell, but I wish he would have. He spoke very quietly and that freaked me out more.

"I didn't cheat on you or anything. I just went to find out more information."

"Why didn't you go through with it?"

"Because it wasn't something I wanted to do. I was doing it because I was desperate. I'm not shaming anyone who wants to enter that profession, but I quickly figured out it wasn't for me. But that's not all."

"Oh?" His question had a tinge of sarcasm to it.

"I came across a tidbit of information that I thought would be my saving grace."

"And what was that?"

"The woman who was interviewing me made a mistake and kept her phone right side up. Someone called her and the name that popped up on her screen was your father, Van Henson." And I stopped talking as I watched Nash angrily pull at his hair.

Before he could say anything, the doorbell ringing stopped our conversation. I looked at the clock and noticed that it wasn't too late, but I wasn't expecting anyone. Nash and I looked at each other. When a loud banging on the door followed, I nearly jumped out of my skin. Nash ran toward the front door before I could even process what had happened. I jogged into the hallway just as he was turning the lock and had reached him just as he was pulling the door open.

Any anger that I felt toward him vanished when the scene in front of me unfolded.

"Who the hell are you?" the man closest to Nash said. He looked somewhat familiar, but I couldn't place him.

Nash clenched his fist. "Who am I? You should be answering that question since you came pounding on this fucking door like you owned it."

"Get out of the way and no one gets hurt. All we need is to talk to Raven."

Nash's roar was enough to send a shiver down my spine. "Fat chance in hell."

This man had two other guys with him and all of them had guns trained on Nash. Nash looked ready to take them all on to protect me. The fact that he was pissed at me mere minutes ago and was ready to burn the whole world down to protect me now, would have made my heart soar under normal circumstances, but this was anything but normal.

A surge of courage flew through me and while some might say that I was being foolish, it seemed like the only way to bring an end to this.

I shook Nash off of me and tossed my body in front of his, taking everyone by surprise. I'd thought I had some scary experiences in my life, but this, by far, was the most frightening.

I could feel Nash trying to pull me behind him, but I wouldn't budge. If he had the opportunity, I knew that he would try to shove me back behind him, but that would cause too much of a distraction. I was worried about it leading to gunfire.

"Stop! He's not trying to hurt me. But, more importantly, who the hell are you?"

"My name is Kingston Cross and I'm your half-brother."

28

NASH

Raven's eyes darted between me and Kingston Cross, who I'd recognized almost immediately. Our families had some similar business interests and ran in the same social circles, so I'd seen him a few times. I was told that Kingston had joined the Chevaliers his freshmen year, just like I had. He'd spoken at a Chevalier meeting my sophomore year. But just because he was a Chevalier, didn't mean I had to trust him wholeheartedly. On the other hand, he didn't have a reason to be here, so it made me even more suspicious. Even though I was pissed at Raven for hiding shit from me, I still promised myself that I would protect her.

"I don't know who the fuck all of you are, and I think you need to leave." I looked over my shoulder and found Raven. Strength radiated off her as she moved out of my shadow. The urge to toss her behind me again in order to protect her with my body was there, but I resisted. This was her moment, her time to show her strength, and I would stand by her but be ready to act if necessary.

It made me think back to when she packed up everything she owned and left town. While she might have thought that it was her being a coward, I now viewed it much differently. Knowing the circumstances under which she made the decision to leave, and followed through with that choice, I saw her actions under the lens of strength. It took a lot of courage to pack up everything you owned and leave town at such a young age. There's no way I would have been able to do the same.

"I can't do that now. I would and have stayed away for this long, but now is the time that you need to learn about your family," Kingston replied.

"You aren't my family. I don't know you at all."

Kingston looked at me before looking back at Raven. "He can confirm to you that I'm Kingston Cross. It would be a waste of my time to be here and lie to you. I have plenty of other things that I could be doing right now."

Raven looked at me and I nodded. I knew that, without a doubt, he was Kingston and he'd made a good point. While I wasn't as familiar with him as I was with Damien, I did know that he was indeed a member of the Cross family. One of the most powerful families in New York City at a minimum, in the entire world at a maximum. There were so many other places he could be that didn't involve him standing in front of us right now.

"That still doesn't make us family."

"Maybe this will help convince you otherwise." He put his hand into the back pocket of his slacks and pulled out a white envelope.

Raven's hand shook as she grabbed the envelope, and she opened it. She pulled out what looked to be an aged piece of paper and gasped. Her eyes became as wide as saucers, and she shook as she handed the piece of paper to me. It was an exact replica of the article she'd shown me earlier with her mom standing with several Cross family members.

"That's my father standing next to your mother in that photo. *Our* father."

Raven shook her head vehemently. "This can't be true."

"We can take a DNA test if that'll help prove to you that none of what I'm saying is a lie. I have plenty of more things to show you, but we need to get out of here now."

That made every warning bell sound in my head. "We aren't going—"

Kingston looked at me with his eyebrow raised, an arrogant smirk lifting the corners of his lips. "You and I both know she's not safe here. After all, that's why you brought her up to the Henson family property right?"

Raven shook beside me and I wanted to knock the smirk right off of his face. Of course he'd known about that, but I found it interesting that he hadn't tried to approach us while we were there. There would have been plenty of opportunities during our week-long stay at my grandfather's cabin, and he didn't take any of them.

"Has there been another threat made against her?"

Kingston nodded. "That's why I'm here with Cross Sentinel, the security company that I own. Pack a quick bag, Raven, and then we'll head out."

Raven looked to me for reassurance, and I nodded, confirming that this arrangement was okay. Deep down, I wondered if I was right, but if this was what we needed to do to keep Raven safe, I was willing to do it. From what I'd known about the Cross family, while they were ruthless, they didn't do things for no reason. There was a reason that Kingston was here, and we needed the information that he had. In order to get it, we needed to go along with his program... for now. But I would be demanding answers very soon.

I went with Raven back to her room, and she quickly tossed things into a bag.

"You know this would be comical if my life wasn't on the line."

"You have a fucked-up sense of humor then. Can I help you?"

Raven chuckled as she said, "Can you grab my laptop?"

"You're taking this way better than I would have expected. A lot of shit just got thrown at you."

"I know, and I'm sure it's the adrenaline that's helping me keep going. I thought something else might happen, but I wasn't sure what. Looks like my gut was right. Are you sure it's okay for us to go with these guys?"

"I don't know them well per se, but my dad does know the entire Cross family. And I know that Kingston is an upstanding member of the Chevaliers so, yes, I think it's something we should do. Plus it will give us time to continue the conversation we were having before we were interrupted."

Raven briefly stopped what she was doing before she responded, "Yes, of course. We do need to do that. I'm—"

"We need to head out now."

Both Raven and I looked toward her doorway and saw Kingston standing there. Raven zipped up her bag and Kingston led the way out of the room and back to the front door. Once we'd made sure her house was locked up tight,

Kingston said, "We'll also make sure that someone is watching the house to make sure that nothing happens to your roommates."

Raven looked at him and said, "Thank you."

There were three black SUVs lined up in a row in front of Raven's house. It was almost like we were about to have our own motorcade. It was then that my eyes reached Landon, who was near an SUV. He gave me a slight nod. Apparently, there was a lot that he and I needed to discuss as well.

Kingston opened up the back of one vehicle and gestured for Raven to get in. When she did, he followed suit behind her and closed the door before I could get in.

Before I could argue, Landon placed a heavy hand on my shoulder and said, "We're going in this one."

I wanted to fight him off, but I knew that the chances of me winning this fight were slim. It was obvious that he was with Kingston's security company, and I would easily get overpowered if I acted out. I needed to play this the smart way instead of rushing into things haphazardly. That would definitely be easier said than done though.

Landon opened the door for me, and I climbed in. He followed behind me and shut the door.

"Where are we going?"

"To one of the Cross Sentinel properties. We'll come back here once we feel that the threat has been dealt with."

"Do you know who is behind this?"

"Put your seatbelt on so we can leave."

I did as he requested. "You're avoiding answering my question."

"We don't know. Their dad had plenty of enemies so it could literally be anyone."

It was still too vague for my liking, but at least it was an answer. I sat back in my chair as our driver pulled away from the curb, immediately behind the car that held Kingston and Raven in it.

The first ten minutes of the drive were made in silence and as the lights grew sparser, it was obvious that we were headed away from Brentson.

"How long is this drive going to be?"

Landon looked up from his phone and said, "Not long."

When I turned my attention back to the vehicle carrying Raven and Kingston, I noticed something strange. Their SUV began to slow up and our driver started to move around theirs.

"What the hell is going on?" I followed Raven's SUV with my eyes and body, shifting myself as we drove past their car.

I didn't need anyone to say a thing because my question was soon answered for me.

After being stopped for several seconds, a huge ball of fire erupted from the SUV, lighting up the night sky.

Panic curled my stomach. There was no way I'd just seen what I thought I had.

"NO!" I yelled. "WHAT THE FUCK?"

The scream felt as if it came from my soul. Going with Kingston Cross willingly had been a huge mistake. I fought against the seatbelt that was restraining me from getting loose. Deep down, I knew there was no way she'd survived the explosion, but it didn't mean that we should keep driving as if it hadn't happened.

I saw Landon pull out his gun and point it at me. Before I could react, he raised the arm holding the gun, quickly brought it down on my head, and everything went black.

THANK YOU FOR READING! The next book in the series, Devious Heir, is available for pre-order now!

WANT MORE of Nash and Raven? I rewrote chapter twelve from his point of view and you can download it HERE.

WANT to join the discussion about the The Brentson University Series? Click HERE to join my Reader Group on Facebook.

PLEASE JOIN my newsletter to find out the latest about the The Ruthless Billionaire Trilogy and my other books!

ABOUT THE AUTHOR

Bri loves a good romance, especially ones that involve a hot anti-hero. That is why she likes to turn the dial up a notch with her own writing. Her Broken Cross series is her debut dark romance series.

She spends most of her time hanging out with her family, plotting her next novel, or reading books by other romance authors.

briblackwood.com

ALSO BY BRI BLACKWOOD

Broken Cross Series

Sinners Empire (Prequel)

Savage Empire

Scarred Empire

Steel Empire

Shadow Empire

Secret Empire

Stolen Empire

The Broken Cross Series Box Set: Books 1-3

The Ruthless Billionaire Trilogy

The Billionaire's Auction

The Billionaire's Possession

The Billionaire's Vengeance

Brentson University Series

Devious Game

Devious Secret

Devious Heir

Merciless Reign Trilogy

Merciless Deception